CRAVE

LONDON VAMPIRES BOOK 2

FELICITY HEATON

First printed July 2019

Second Edition

Layout and design by Felicity Heaton

THE LONDON VAMPIRES SERIES

Book 1: Covet

Book 2: Crave

Book 3: Seduce

Book 4: Enslave

Book 5: Bewitch

Book 6: Unleash

Discover more available paranormal romance books at:
http://www.felicityheaton.com

Or sign up to my mailing list to receive a FREE vampire romance ebook, learn about new titles, be eligible for special subscriber-only giveaways, and read exclusive content including short stories:
http://ml.felicityheaton.com/mailinglist

CHAPTER 1

Three weeks had passed since Callum had left London and headed to Paris to scout for performers for a new show at the theatre he ran with three other vampires, and it had been one week since he had last emailed Antoine, the aristocrat pureblood in charge of overseeing the performances at Vampirerotique.

He should have contacted him again by now. It wasn't as though Callum hadn't thought about it. He had booted up his laptop and started to type out the email every morning before retiring for the day. Yesterday, he had even reached the point of typing in his name at the end of the email before deleting the entire thing.

Callum leaned his back against the brass rail that edged the curved dark mahogany bar top, his green gaze scanning the occupants of the crowded room, picking out viable prey, potential performers, and identifying the species of each person his eyes fell on.

Part of him was still working and it was that part that kept whispering that Antoine wouldn't be angry with him for disappearing.

If he just dropped a brief email or even a text message stating that he was still looking for performers but hadn't spotted anyone worthy of joining the Vampirerotique family in the past week then Antoine would probably forgive him for disobeying his command to contact him daily.

It would be a lie though.

He had seen several vampires, both male and female, at the nightclubs he had been moving between for the past three weeks.

All of them would work well in the theatre and draw the crowds.

They were exhibitionists who had been more than comfortable performing private acts in front of the gathered dancers. There had been males who had groped and grinded with their human female prey, and female vampires who had engaged in acts just a whisper away from screwing in the open booths where anyone could see them.

All of them had been worthy of him approaching them and giving them the hard sell.

Not many of their type refused to audition when they gained an all expenses paid trip to London and the chance to try out for a place in a famous theatre.

There was one female who had stood out amongst the usual crowd last week. She was perfect for the new show that Antoine had in mind, could easily be the star performer, but Callum couldn't bring himself to approach her and whenever he thought about mentioning her to Antoine, a knot formed deep in his gut.

Callum had ignored the feeling and just satisfied himself with watching her in the club. He had first seen her with another female, one that he had approached during a lull towards the end of the evening. She had eagerly accepted his offer of an audition, even though she knew the sort of place his theatre was and that it didn't normally look for performers from her species.

Werewolf.

When Antoine had first told him that he would be departing for Paris in search of new talent, and that it wouldn't just be the usual scouting mission this time but would include seeking werewolves for a special performance, Callum had almost choked on his glass of blood.

Vampirerotique had never hired werewolves before. In fact, he was certain that in the hundred years they had been running the theatre, there had never been a werewolf on stage. Their kind rarely interacted with each other, unless you counted the occasional war. Werewolves didn't like vampires. The feeling was more than mutual.

Callum had sent three werewolves to audition so far, all female as requested.

This female would be perfect for the show too. She would steal it and make it hers, just as she stole the attention of the entire club as she moved through it with sensual grace that had the eyes of every male and some females on her, and made Callum think about some therianthropes he had met in the past. She had the moves of a feline shifter rather than a werewolf.

Callum could easily imagine her moving on the stage, how she would sidle over to the large vampire males and bring them to their knees with only a seductive sway of her hips and flash of a sultry smile.

Hell, she had Callum on his knees. He had been following her for a week now, shunning his duty in favour of tracking her down each night and watching her from a distance.

His new private pleasure.

The club she had chosen tonight catered to a mixed crowd, although the humans didn't know that.

One of the male bartenders was a shifter, one was human, and one was a vampire.

That surprised Callum.

He had never thought he would live to see a vampire working alongside a shifter, but the two young males seemed to get along. He couldn't sense any bad feelings between them so it wasn't an act put on for the sake of the patrons and the human bartender.

Callum's gaze tracked the female through the club, studying how she slid between the dancers, occasionally stopping to work her body against a male.

She smiled wickedly at a young human man as he caught her wrist and pulled her against him, twisting her so her back pressed against his front.

She wriggled her hips and raised her hands above her head as she slid down the length of her partner and then back up again, almost as tall as he was in her heeled black boots. Her tight dark jeans emphasised lean long legs that Callum had rather disturbingly dreamed about since first seeing her, imagining their slender strong lengths wrapped around his backside as he fucked her.

He had dreamed about pushing the loose flowing material of her empire-line top up to reveal the toned plane of her stomach and then kissing it, feeling her body shift beneath him, before continuing and peeling the high waist tucked under her breasts over their full firm globes. He had dipped his head and captured each sweet dusky bud in turn, swirling his tongue around and sucking them until she moaned low in appreciation.

The brunette female werewolf moved on, thanking her temporary partner with a brief brush of her rosy lips across his cheek and a saucy stroke of her palm over his crotch that had Callum ready to speed onto the dance floor and rip the human to shreds.

She was his.

He drew a long slow breath to calm himself, focusing on it and not her, waiting for the need to pass. If he looked at her now, he would be on the dance floor before he realised what he was doing and would be tugging her into his arms, using all of his strength to make it clear to her that she belonged to him now.

Callum shook his head to rid it of the desire to dance with her and feel her body pressing into his, hot and supple under his questing hands. He wouldn't let her go as easily as the male human had.

He watched her move through the dancers again, twirling and smiling, her wavy soft brown hair dancing with her, tumbling over her shoulders and breasts. Each time she lifted her bare arms in the air, the hem of her top rose, revealing a tantalising flash of her stomach or back. Her jeans rode low on her hips, barely covering her backside and crotch.

She was a vixen, a real predator as she glanced over every man, even those with partners, looking for tonight's fun. He had seen her leave with a new man every night.

A strange urge to follow her and see what she did with them had built inside him until he had no longer been able to resist the need to know.

It wasn't what he had thought it would be and an even stranger feeling had swept through him on realising that she was luring males away to feed on them.

Like his kind, werewolves enjoyed the taste of blood and needed it to survive, although they could supplement their need with nourishment from food.

Unlike his kind, werewolves couldn't turn a human. Her bite wouldn't change the human into a werewolf. Once she had finished with the man, she had wiped his memory and left him in the alley.

Callum had almost followed her home but had forced himself to return to his hotel instead. The sight of her feeding had given him some seriously erotic dreams and he had woken tonight with a raging erection that hadn't gone down until he had tended to it.

It was coming back as he watched her, his thoughts diving down routes they shouldn't be taking. A vampire had no place desiring a werewolf.

Desiring?

Hell, this hunger went beyond desire and ran deeper in his veins than lust.

He craved her.

Callum turned and flagged down the vampire bartender. The blond man smiled knowingly, nodded, and took down a martini glass. He filled it to the brim with dark liquid that was black in the flashing purple and blue lights of the club and stuck a cherry on a stick in it.

Callum held out a twenty euro note at the same time as the vampire placed the glass down on an elegant white napkin and slid it across the bar to him.

"I'll take one of those," a female voice said right beside him, "and tall, dark and sexy here is paying."

He was?

Callum frowned and turned to say that he damn well wasn't paying for her drink and froze as his eyes fell on the female werewolf. He felt the vampire bartender's gaze on him, sensed him waiting to see what Callum's reply would be. Callum glanced at him and nodded.

The vampire made up another glass of blood, stuck a cherry in it, and slid it over to her before moving away.

The werewolf raised her glass in a salute to Callum, sipped the blood, and set it back down on the napkin. Her bloodstained lips curved into a wicked sultry smile.

Callum was smitten.

She leaned closer, her bare left elbow resting on the bar, and ran her fingertips down his dark purple silk tie. Her smile widened when she curled her fingers around it, drew it away from his black tailored shirt, and tugged him towards her.

"You've been watching me like I'm a bitch in heat and you're an alpha. What gives?" She wasn't French as he had expected.

Her accent was as British as his own.

Callum calmly removed her hand from his tie, straightened it out and smoothed it down. "I'm just here on business, and I'm definitely not an alpha. I'm a vampire."

She smiled and tilted her head to one side, causing the long waves of her brown hair to shift across her breasts and cover the tempting display of cleavage the tight section of her black sleeveless top created.

"A vampire with a definite hard-on for a species most of his kind would see as disgusting and forbidden," she said over the rapid beat of the music, lifted the cocktail stick and cherry from her drink, and popped it into her mouth.

Callum's gaze narrowed on her mouth, transfixed by the sight of her sucking the cherry.

She parted her lips and withdrew the glossy red fruit, dipped it back into her blood and swirled it around before raising it back to her mouth and teasing him by licking the crimson liquid off it again.

His chest tightened and he struggled to breathe as the tip of her tongue flicked over the cherry, swirling around it.

She slowly slid the fruit into her mouth, lips puckering as she sucked, her eyes closing in what looked like pleasure to him.

The sight of her ratcheted his hunger up another notch, flooding him with a deep throbbing ache to feel her tongue brushing his in the way it had the cherry, to have her mouth on his flesh and to run his lips over every inch of her bare skin and drive her wild until she was sobbing his name and begging for more.

"I don't have a hard-on for your species... just you." Callum moved faster than she could evade, catching the wrist of the hand she held the cocktail stick in, pulling it away from her lips and claiming them for his own.

She responded instantly, her tongue thrusting past his lips and teeth to slide along his. He slanted his head, slipped his other arm around her slim waist and dragged the full length of her body against his as he seized control of the kiss.

She melted against him, as supple and hot as he had dreamed she would be, her breasts pressing into his hard chest, the heat of her driving him to the edge.

He tangled his tongue with hers, swallowing her breathy gasps as he dominated her, crushing each attempt she made to reclaim control. Her fight only made him burn hotter for her, made him use his strength on her and tighten his grip on her wrist and side.

Her gasps became low rumbling moans.

The firmer he was with her, the more of his strength he used, the lower they became and the more she struggled, as though she wanted to feel how much more powerful he was than her.

She liked it.

The female werewolf snapped out of his grasp and slapped him so hard across his cheek that he couldn't fail to realise where he had gone wrong.

His fangs cut into his lower lip.

He hadn't noticed them extending.

Before he could explain to her that it was just the heat of the moment that had brought them out and that he hadn't intended to bite her, she was striding away from him, heading back towards the busy dance floor.

Callum growled, swiftly drank his martini glass of blood to take the edge off his hunger and followed her, intent on explaining and tasting her again.

The crowd kept closing behind her, blocking his way and frustrating him.

He pushed through them, his senses tracking her so he didn't lose her again.

She wasn't heading out of the club at least. The expansive dark club only had one exit and that was the other way, beyond the bar. She was either heading towards the booths that lined the edges of the room or the dance floor itself.

Was she planning on losing him in the throng of people?

It would be difficult to track her in amongst so many signatures. There were several other werewolves in the club tonight. Their presence would help mask hers even though he knew her scent now, had instinctively put it to memory when kissing her. Devil, she had tasted so wicked and delicious.

Callum licked the faint trace of blood off his lips and finally broke through the crowd around the bar, coming out near the edge of the dance floor. The heavy beat of the music pounded through his body, thrumming in his veins, pushing the tension mounting inside him, the need to find her and have her in his arms again.

The need to taste her lips.

He scoured the dancers and spotted her heading closer to the DJ. The lights flashed brightest there, hurting his eyes, and the volume of the music would be unbearable that close to the speakers.

She knew vampires well.

Her species could move around during the day so they weren't as sensitive to light and her hearing wasn't as acute when she was in her human form. She stopped there and danced with a male.

He couldn't tell whether her partner was human or werewolf, but he was immense, taller and broader than Callum was.

She had intentionally chosen a place that would hurt him and had now selected a partner who could easily protect her. Her wiliness told Callum that the male would be a werewolf.

He only wondered why she no longer looked confident. Her gaze constantly darted about as she danced with the man, her body held at a distance from his, as though she was afraid to get any closer. Why would she fear her own kind?

That question and the challenge she had issued by choosing to dance with an immense werewolf in an area that was uncomfortable for Callum drove him onto the dance floor.

He moved through the crowd, his gaze constantly on her, studying her face and the flicker of fear that was gradually surfacing in her eyes. The usual confident shine in them was gone by the time he was within a few metres of her.

The male werewolf caught her shoulders, turned her around and dragged her back against his bulky body, caging her there with a thick forearm across her stomach.

His black t-shirt stretched over an obscene amount of muscle and Callum considered the insanity of approaching such a male. Although he was likely older than the werewolf, and vampires were inherently more powerful, his build was almost slender compared to him and he was a good few inches shorter too.

That could be an advantage though.

A lower centre of gravity gave him a more solid footing than his monolithic rival and his slimmer build gave him the advantage of speed. He could probably incapacitate the werewolf with only minimal injury to himself.

However.

There were two other male werewolves seated on the curved dark leather seat of the booth behind the male dancing with the woman, and both of them were watching the couple. Three glasses stood on the oval black table in the centre of the booth. The male was with them.

One werewolf he might be able to handle.

Three would crush him.

It should have stopped him from pursuing the woman, but his feet still propelled him forwards, towards what could only be a bloody and painful future.

He couldn't turn back now that he had tasted her.

He hungered for another touch, another taste.

He craved her.

And he would have her.

CHAPTER 2

What was she doing?

When she had fled England, Kristina had vowed to avoid interacting with werewolves. It was safest that way, no matter how much she often craved the company of her kind.

All packs had a unique scent, something a werewolf could smell on each other and recognise. Part of her training as a cub had been spent on burning knowledge of the European werewolf packs and their scents into her mind. It was something all packs taught their young.

The man now grinding against her backside and turning her stomach with his dominant grip on her was from a local pack here in Paris but that didn't mean he wouldn't turn her over.

She had been on the run from her pack for months now but she was sure they were still looking for her.

This was a mistake.

Kristina tried to get free of her partner but his thick arm tightened across her stomach, holding her firm.

A spark of panic leapt through her blood and she struggled to tamp it down and disguise it so he wouldn't sense it in her. She made out she was turning in his arms and he allowed it, his large hands moving to her backside, clutching and squeezing.

What the Hell had she been thinking?

The vampire had scared her and she had gone running to her own kind.

Pathetic.

She was stronger than that.

So his fangs had come out and she had felt their sharp tips on her tongue, that didn't mean he had intended to bite her.

Not everything she had been told about vampires was true.

She had thought she had known that, had accepted it as fact, and had always been proud of herself for being able to see that vampires weren't really a threat unless you made them one by provoking them.

It turned out that she was wrong and she hadn't accepted it after all.

The moment his fangs had touched her, she had panicked and lashed out, her heart rocketing and hackles rising.

Everything bad she had ever been told about vampires had shot through her mind and she had gone with it rather than telling herself that it was just desire that had brought his fangs out.

It was a reaction her kind shared with vampires. Whenever she got a little overexcited, her canines extended against her will.

She should have been flattered by his reaction to her kiss, not sought to knock his fangs out.

She was no better than every other werewolf. They had driven fear of vampires, horror stories about them, so deep into her mind that she couldn't escape it even when she thought that she had.

The male werewolf leaned down towards her and she stiffened in his arms, fear of him rising inside her and telling her to break away from him, that he would try to dominate her just as her alpha had. She had to run.

His warm breath washed over her skin, turning her stomach, and she shrank backwards, trying to escape his touch.

She had been a fool to run back to her own kind for protection. She had probably been safer with the vampire than she was with this male.

They all wanted the same thing from her, all smelt her readiness to mate and took it to mean that she wanted them when she didn't. She wasn't interested in bearing cubs like a dutiful female. She wanted a life.

A firm cool hand on her shoulder caused her to jump. The start of a shriek escaped her before she clamped down hard on it and the world whirled past her in a blur of blue and purple neon and laser lights.

A hard wall of black slammed against her and a low threatening snarl curled out over the pumping music.

Her instincts sparked, senses zeroing in on the male werewolf at her back and the dark presence of vampire in front of her.

The vampire's arm tightened around her, pressing her to his chest, and he snarled again, a feral sound that a werewolf would have been proud of making.

The werewolf growled back but it lacked the strength and ferocity of the vampire's, sounding weak and tailing off at the end.

Kristina glanced up at her unlikely saviour, looking past the strong defined line of his jaw and the sensual mouth that had sent her head spinning with only a kiss, beyond his straight nose that said he might be an aristocrat vampire, to the red coals of his irises and the vertical slits of his pupils.

He growled again, bearing his fangs.

They were enormous now, fully extended as he threatened the werewolf behind her.

The werewolf snarled back at him and she sensed the two other male werewolves rise from their seats, heading out of the booth to back up their leader.

Kristina wasn't sure how to defuse the situation before it exploded. She did the first thing that came to her.

She tiptoed, caught the vampire's cheek in her palm, and kissed him.

The werewolves behind her stopped moving.

The vampire froze against her, his mouth slack and unmoving.

With all four males shocked, Kristina made her move.

She grabbed the vampire's hand, twisted out of his embrace, and dragged him into the crowd. They had made it halfway across the dance floor before she heard the werewolf growl and felt the vampire come back to his senses.

His hand shifted in hers and he spun her into his arms. He looked down at her, the flicker of coloured lights over his face turning his eyes from red to blue to purple and back again.

Kristina expected him to shout at her, or try to escape her grasp and return to fight the werewolf, or do something.

He just stood there in the middle of the dance floor staring at her.

His pupils gradually widened, switching back to their normal state, and the colour of his irises shifted, so the lights now made them flicker between green, blue and purple.

"I wasn't going to bite you," he said in a low voice that she barely heard over the music and stepped towards her, until she could sense his body close to hers and the temptation to move the bare few inches and bring them against each other hummed through her. "But he was."

The hard look that entered his emerald eyes caused her to divert hers and she stared past him, not wanting to admit that he was right and the male werewolf had intended to mark her right there in front of everyone and she had been too weak and scared to do anything about it.

"What's your name?" she whispered and shoved her weakness away, cleared her throat, lifted her chin and looked directly into his eyes. "I think I have a right to know the name of my hero."

"Hero?" He laughed and shook his head, causing a silken strand of his long black hair to drift down against his cheek. He casually swept it back behind his ear, so it curled around it, and then smiled at her. "I'm hardly the good guy here... but you can call me Callum."

Callum. Cal.

Although he didn't look like the sort of man who would easily accept someone shortening his name without permission.

Kristina bravely closed the gap between them and ran her hands over the soft black cotton of his obviously expensive shirt. His chest was granite hard beneath the material, the feel of it sending a hum of pleasure through her body as she recalled the strength of his grip when he had kissed her and when he had rescued her from one of her own kind.

She slid her palms up to his strong broad shoulders, looped them around his neck, and started to move against him.

He kept perfectly still, the calm confidence in his eyes melting away to allow something akin to confusion to surface.

"Well, Callum." She tipped her head back and looked up into his eyes. They were locked on hers, searching, probing, as though hers might tell him what she was up to and what she intended to get out of him by swaying in his arms. His pupils dilated with the first brush of her hips across his and his bowed lips parted to reveal the barest trace of straight white teeth. "Don't you want to know my name?"

Kristina rotated her hips into his and held her nerve when she felt the growing bulge in his black trousers. He looked beautifully startled when she pressed her groin against his, moving up and down his body, teasing him with the friction.

The hunger for him that had begun as little more than a spark of interest when she had noticed him watching her around six days ago had slowly grown into a burning desire for him three days ago and she had been teasing him since then, toying with him. She had wanted to speak to him so many times so she could know why he watched her so closely and why he was following her.

Her initial reaction had been one of fear but then she had realised that he was a vampire, not one of her alpha's goons come to take her home. The feel of his eyes on her had given her confidence that she had never felt before. She had danced with men, aware that he was watching, putting on a show for him.

Her nightly repertoire had grown in the strange pre-dawn twilight this morning, climaxing in her feeding on a human man while he watched from the shadows.

When she had stepped away from the man and wiped his mind of the incident, replacing the memories with ones of passion, she had felt sure that the vampire would make his move, that the sight of her feeding would have driven him over the edge.

He had stayed in the shadows for long minutes and then left.

Had he fought his desire and won?

Part of her despised him for that, for having better control than she had over herself. She hadn't been able to overcome her curiosity tonight and had gone to him, only to run away like a cub when she had felt his fangs. Well, that wouldn't happen again.

Kristina wiggled her way back up him, twirled the long black hair in the ponytail at the nape of his neck, and smiled into his eyes, giving him her best seductive look.

His pupils dilated further and he finally moved, his hands coming to settle on her hips and then sliding upwards to the low waist of her tight jeans. She shivered with the first caress of his cool palms over her waist, his hands under the flowing loose material of her top.

His thumbs pressed into her stomach, fingers firm against her back, the touch electrifying her.

It was dominant but in the best way. He was reconfirming his strength and silently telling her that he could easily take control of things if he wanted, while his expression told her that he was also more than happy to comply and let her take the lead.

She swayed her hips and moved down his body again, trailing her palms over his shoulders and chest, forcing his hands on her up to her ribs and the sides of her breasts. His eyes narrowed briefly, heat blazing in them as he shifted his hands forwards to capture her breasts, and then he frowned when she worked her way upwards again before he could touch them.

He stepped into her, wedging a hard muscular thigh between her legs and stopping her from wriggling. A moan slipped from her lips as he moved it, brushing it against her groin, and she looped her arms around his neck.

Staring into his eyes, lost in them, she forgot about the werewolves in the club and the pack back in England that were searching for her.

The world fell away, taking her cares with it, stripping her of the part of her that continually whispered that this man was not for her.

It didn't matter that he was handsome and strong. It didn't matter that when he watched her she felt as though she could do anything. It didn't matter that she wanted him more than was reasonable and that her need for him was fierce and controlled her to a degree.

He was a vampire.

In his arms like this, that was the thing that no longer mattered.

He bent towards her, his hands pressing into her sides as he lowered them down from her waist over her hips and round to her backside. He pulled her closer, cranking her temperature up another ten degrees, and moved against her.

The slide of his thigh between hers, the fleeting contact between his hard body and her aching one, had her sinking her teeth into her lower lip.

She wanted more, cursed her tight jeans for inhibiting her and stopping her from being able to gain the satisfaction she desired. She pushed against him, curling her hips, hungry and seeking more friction to sate her need.

Callum's cool skin brushing her neck startled her and her gaze leapt from his to what she could see of his hand out of the corner of her eye. He swept the tangled lengths of her hair from her throat, the teasing whisper of his fingers over her hungry body almost too much for her to bear, and then leaned into her.

Kristina moaned and couldn't stop herself from tilting her head to one side even though she was aware that by doing so she was breaking the rules of her kind. It was wrong of her to welcome a vampire's touch and let him kiss her throat, especially when she had feared one of her own species doing such a thing to her just minutes before.

It was different with Callum.

The hard press of his lips on her throat, the sweep of his tongue over her jugular, stirred only desire in her, flooding her with the ache to bury her fingers into his hair and anchor him there so he wouldn't stop.

There was no threat in his caress, no sense that he intended to sink his fangs into her, and even if he did, it would only be the vampire equivalent of a love bite.

The werewolf had intended to mark her and claim her with the bite.

A vampire couldn't do such a thing.

"Tell me your name," Callum husked into her ear, his cool breath tickling her skin.

He kissed and sucked her earlobe, curled his tongue around it, sending a shiver down her throat that set her aflame. She rocked against him, meeting his shallow thrusts, panting as her desire got the better of her. His firm grip on her backside with one hand and the nape of her neck with the other drove her wild.

She bucked and writhed, rubbing herself along the length of his thigh. Her fingertips pressed into the hard bulge of his pectorals and raked downwards, catching his nipples through his black shirt and tearing a groan from him. She answered him with a moan of her own when she reached the granite slab of his stomach, her imagination running away with her.

What would he look like nude and in all his glory?

She pictured a lean built physique. Muscles that could melt a woman right down to her core barely hidden beneath milky skin. A trail of hair as dark as his ponytail that led down from the sensual dip of his navel to his impressive hard cock. Lithe powerful legs that exuded strength as much as the rest of him. He was a god in her imagination.

Would he be that way in reality?

She had an itch to find out and wanted to scratch it right there in the club.

"Tell me," he said again, voice rough with desire, and nipped her earlobe.

It was hard to think when he was licking and kissing, his body moving into hers, hands grasping and kneading. She couldn't remember her own name. All she knew was intense pleasure and a craving for more.

He chuckled against her throat and kissed it again, wet open mouthed ones that made the fragments of thoughts she had gathered scatter and tore a moan from her.

"I guess I'm not the only one having trouble functioning here." His voice was a silken purr in her ear and he suddenly stepped away from her.

Kristina stood on jelly legs, gripping the sleeves of his black shirt in tight fists to keep herself upright. He looked around them and enough sense broke through the haze of arousal fogging her mind for her to wonder what he was looking for.

She stumbled when he locked a strong hand around her wrist and strode towards the edge of the dance floor. She bumped into several dancers, mumbling apologies, and saw past Callum's wide shoulders.

A couple exited one of the curtained booths directly ahead of them.

A blush blazed across her cheeks as she realised what he was up to and what might happen between them if she entered the private booth with him and sense reared its ugly head and told her to break free of him before it was too late.

The desire to do such a thing faltered and died when he looked over his shoulder at her, his hungry gaze devouring hers, expressing everything that she was feeling inside. He knew as well as she did that this was wrong but it wasn't stopping him.

And she wouldn't let it stop her either.

He pulled her into the booth, closed the heavy black velvet curtains with one stroke, and turned on her.

Kristina let her breath out on a sigh as he claimed her waist, moulded her body against the hard expanse of his, and kissed her.

Before she started to kiss him back, before things got beyond her control and she lost her ability to think again, she pulled away and stared into his eyes.

"Kristina," she breathed and he grinned sexily.

"Now I know what to call you when I lose myself in you."

Oh, Heavens, that sounded so hot husked in his deep voice as he stared at her with hungry eyes that promised he wouldn't let her go until he had satisfied the passion bouncing between them.

Kristina grabbed his tie, yanked him to her and pressed a brief hard kiss to his lips.

She smiled wickedly.

"Mister, you'll be screaming it by the time I'm done with you."

CHAPTER 3

Callum backed her up until her calves hit the curved leather seat of the booth and she fell onto her bottom. He towered over her, immense and beautiful, dark and deadly, just the sight of him exciting her. Kristina tried to stand again but he pressed his right hand to her shoulder and forced her back onto the seat.

He tugged at the knot of his dark purple tie and loosened it before slipping the two sides free of each other. His fingers started on the buttons of his black shirt next and a tiny seed of fear settled in the pit of her stomach, took root, and started to grow.

"We should take this somewhere a little more private," she said automatically and he paused at his work, his fingers halfway down his chest and the top part of his shirt open to reveal the groove between his pectorals.

Hell, it was hard not to pounce on him and screw him right there on the tacky dirty booth floor.

Her gaze stayed rooted on the tiny patch of his chest that she could see, her body willing her to give up the false sense of propriety that had suddenly claimed her and just reach out and take what she wanted.

Callum.

Vampire.

His fingers started their work again and she itched to reach up and join them in revealing his body to her hungry eyes.

"This is private enough," he husked in a passion roughened voice and smiled reassuringly. "No one will disturb us."

She wasn't so sure.

There were three male werewolves who had seen her kiss the vampire, and watched them on the dance floor and then exit it for this booth, and one of them had a big old dent in his masculine pride that needed fixing.

Male werewolves were ridiculously hard-headed and primal. She didn't want to look up halfway through scratching her itch for Callum to find a glowering werewolf looming over them.

"I can't hold out until we find somewhere else." Callum's low spoken words barely reached her over the pounding beat of the music but they struck a chord in her.

She raked her gaze over him, burning at a thousand degrees for the cool feel of his hands on her bare body and his mouth claiming hers again. Who was she kidding? She felt the same way. She wouldn't last until her hotel. If they took a cab, she would probably end up riding him in the backseat for the driver to see. She was running too hot now to turn back.

Kristina grabbed the two sides of the tie resting around his neck, dragged him down to his knees before her, and kissed him again.

His tongue thrust into her mouth, cool and dominant, sliding over hers in the most delicious way. The feel of his hands on her thighs and the way they shifted roughly to her backside and tugged her to the edge of the leather seat sent a quiver through her and flooded her mind with images of him using his strength on her in other ways.

She shivered at the vision of him grasping her wrists in one hand and sinking his long cock into her, thrusting wildly until they were both sweaty and hot, both gasping for air and exploding with need.

She bit his lower lip and sucked it into her mouth. He groaned and clutched her backside tighter, clawing at her through the denim. Devil, she wanted him inside her now. She tore at his fancy shirt, not caring that she was wrecking it. She would do the same to his trousers next. She wanted him naked and bucking against her.

Fevered and desperate, she grumbled as she reached his waist and tugged the shirt out. Callum growled when she ripped the two sides apart, sending buttons flying and pinging around the booth.

He kissed her deeper, rough and hungry, his mouth hard against hers and tongue thrusting and warring with hers. She twisted her fingers in his long black hair, holding him tightly to her mouth, and went to work on his belt with her other hand.

It was undone in the blink of an eye and her hand went straight to his fly.

Callum groaned, tore away from her, and snarled as he undid his trousers for her, shoving them down around his thighs.

She didn't get a chance to catch a glimpse of his erection.

The next thing she saw was the dark ceiling of the club as her back hit the seat, her bottom hanging off it and supported by Callum. The ceiling flashed purple and blue as the lights bounced in time with the pounding music. Callum ripped her jeans open, hooked his fingers into the waist at her hips, and whipped them down to her knees.

His irritated growl made her smile.

Boots.

They were laced too.

She was surprised he didn't just tear her jeans in half to get at her.

The vision of him doing such a thing thrilled her. He set to work on one boot and when Kristina realised that it was going to take too long for him to get them both off her and she didn't want to wait, she sat up and ran a claw up the laces of her other boot and shoved it off.

Callum stared wide eyed at what she had done and then did the same to her other boot, using his claws to cut through the laces.

Kristina wriggled on the seat, her panties wet through with need, burning for Callum. He got her jeans off and then grabbed the sides of her underwear. She shuffled to the edge of the couch and pulled her top off over her head as he dealt with her underwear. Her heart pounded at the thought of being caught completely naked by someone but she needed to feel Callum's bare chest against hers.

His eyes darkened as they found her bare breasts and he palmed them, thumbing her hard nipples. Tingles and shivers danced outwards from their centres and she couldn't take it. Not this time. She wasn't looking for foreplay. She needed Callum inside her, had been burning to feel him against her, taking her, all week.

Kristina kissed him again, rough and passionate, a clashing of lips and tongues, and then broke away and looked down between them. His cock was as impressive as she had imagined. She trailed her fingers down the dark line of hair that joined his navel to his erection and then curled her fingers around the granite hard length and squeezed.

Callum hissed through his teeth and clenched his jaw, his eyes screwed shut. When they opened again, meeting hers, they were darker than ever, flooded with desire and need that echoed inside her.

He claimed her backside, yanked her to the edge of the seat, and sank his cock into her wet sheath in one hard thrust. Kristina cried into his neck, hands grasping his strong shoulders, and breathed hard.

The sting of pain from his swift entry faded as he withdrew and she gasped when he thrust back in, deeper than before, filling her completely.

She wrapped her legs around his backside and clung to him as he pumped her hard and fast, frenzied thrusts that still weren't enough for her. Her heart beat wildly, body quivering with need only he could sate, and she kissed and licked his neck.

His fingers tightened against her bare bottom, digging in, holding her fast as he curled his hips into hers, plunging his long cock hard into her. She rode his passion, matching him strength for strength, not letting him best her. She could take more if he wanted to give it to her.

He groaned when she planted her feet back on the ground and moved off the edge of the seat so she could meet him thrust for thrust. Her calves ached as she supported herself with his help and bore down on him each time he thrust upwards, so their bodies met hard and his cock was sheathed to the hilt.

Kristina kissed him messily each time their bodies met, stealing a brush of his lips or sweep of his tongue. She grasped handfuls of his hair and curled her pelvis, forcing the length of his rigid cock along her sweetest spot.

A gasp broke her lips with each delicious plunge of his body into hers that sent a flash of heat blazing through her.

It all settled in her abdomen, tightening it until she couldn't control herself anymore and wildly reached for her climax with him.

He muttered her name against her lips and her throat as he kissed and devoured them with his mouth, and she tilted her head back. She couldn't take any more.

It felt too good.

Just one more thrust.

One more.

Callum pinned her backside against the seat, held her so tightly that it hurt, and bucked hard into her warm core. His pelvis slammed into her clit.

Heat blazed outwards.

The world shattered.

Kristina slumped forwards, laid her head on his shoulder, and breathed fast in time with him. His cock throbbed inside her, his balls shifting against her backside. She draped her arms around him, tired and sated, the fog of desire slowly melting away from her mind and reality gradually creeping back.

She closed her eyes to shut the world out and imagined them somewhere else, somewhere away from the grotty nightclub and the danger of werewolves. Somewhere she could do this all over again.

And again.

He withdrew from her and his seed trickled downwards, warm now but it chilled her to a degree. A vampire couldn't get a werewolf pregnant as far as she knew, but she was ripe for mating and she didn't really know him.

She should have been more cautious.

Kristina drew in a slow breath to steady the pounding of her heart and expelled it, pushing out her fear with it.

She fixed a smile on her face and sat back, still astride Callum's thighs, her back against the seat edge.

"Did you scream my name?" she said and his serious look melted into a smile.

"I think so. It all went a little hazy there for a moment." Callum leaned in and kissed her, softer this time, almost lazy, as though they had been lovers for a long time and this was more than a one night stand. "You screamed mine."

She had?

Kristina couldn't remember that.

The whole universe had exploded when she had climaxed.

She might have shouted it.

If she had, he had deserved it. The man screwed like a bucking bronco. A flash of heat swept over her skin, setting her finer hairs on end, and she kissed him again to satisfy her returning hunger for him. This wasn't going to happen again, no matter how much she still burned to feel him against her.

He palmed her breasts, his cool fingers teasing the buds of her nipples, reigniting her desire. She slowed the kiss to match the pace of his caress and ran her hands over his shoulders. This wasn't happening again. No.

No.

Kristina moaned as his tongue entered her mouth, sliding along the length of hers, his taste flooding her senses. She shifted her hips to satisfy some of the returning ache there and he lowered his hand, delved his fingers between her plush petals, and found her aroused nub. She gasped as he teased it, swirling his fingers and then pinching, sending sparks shooting.

He eased his hand downwards and inserted two fingers into her sheath, pumping her slowly with them while his other hand continued to tease her breasts and his mouth worked lazily against hers.

She tried and failed to tell herself to make him stop.

Just one more time.

Just like this.

She wouldn't give in to her desire to have his body buried in hers again, thrusting and plunging, driving her wild, but she would let this happen. Images of them entwined and naked, writhing against each other on a large bed flashed across her closed eyes, interspersed with visions of them in this booth, her bent over forwards as he took her from behind, his long cock filling her and scratching her persistent itch for him.

Kristina worked her hips, riding his fingers, and he lowered his other hand to tease her clit, circling and squeezing. He swallowed her gasps, moaning after each one, as though the sound of them and the feel of her body clenching his fingers and straining for another orgasm pleasured him.

Her hands clutched his shoulders and she lost herself in the moment, in the rhythmic plunge of his fingers into her core and the way they rubbed the softer spot just inside, taking her higher and higher.

She moaned and shivered, tightened her sheath around his fingers, eager for release that remained frustratingly out of her reach.

"Kristina," he murmured into her mouth and she moaned, unable to form a real response or find her voice while he was fucking her with his fingers.

Devil, she couldn't stop imagining where all this could lead.

She pictured herself riding his face, feeling his tongue sliding over her clit and then dipping into her core. She imagined him pinning her against a wall as he took her, backside tensing as he pumped her hard and fast.

She moaned and kept imagining everything she could do with him, letting her mind delve down wicked routes involving handcuffs and blindfolds, feathers and lubricant.

Each brush of his fingertips over her clit and thrust of his two fingers into her core brought new images, new positions, and added fuel to the fire within her, until she knew she couldn't let this end here tonight. She needed him too much to let it be just one night of madness.

She had never needed a man like this.

None of her past lovers had set her aflame like Callum had, or had matched her strength and passion, or sent her mind racing to dream of things she had never tried before, wicked sensual things she had only read about in books.

"Callum," she whispered, rotating her hips, urging him to give her release.

She reached down and wasn't surprised to find that his cock was hard again, heavy and eager as he thrust it through the ring of her fingers.

He groaned and pumped into her hand, as though he was screwing it. The feel of him bucking into it filled her with a need to see it. She wanted to see him thrusting, wanted to watch him fuck her hand in the same way he had taken her just minutes before.

It turned her on, sending her arousal soaring.

She wanted to see his beautiful cock as it would have been moving inside her, giving her undeniable pleasure and incredible satisfaction.

Callum moaned again when she tightened her grip, his hips thrusting roughly, his fingers moving deeper and more desperately inside her. He screwed his face up, frowning hard, his teeth clenched together. Kristina moved her hand on him, fascinated by the sight of him, thrilled by it and aching to feel him filling her up again.

"Wait," he whispered and pulled his hips back. He breathed hard. His fingers paused inside her. His eyes opened, their sharp green irises meeting hers, and he frowned. "Let me come inside you again... Christ... I need to."

Kristina tensed.

She needed it too but she was already a mess as it was and the thought of pregnancy still plagued her. She wanted to feel him throbbing with his release though, wanted to know she had given him the same addictive brand of pleasure he had given to her.

"Do you have..." She felt stupid so cut herself off.

The damage was probably done already if it was a possibility, but she didn't need to encourage her body into accepting him as a mate.

Werewolves and vampires hated each other.

What would happen if she fell pregnant from this encounter and produced a hybrid child?

Callum would probably want nothing to do with it, and it was hard enough being a werewolf on the run, let alone adding single mother to that burden.

Callum's frown hardened and then his eyebrows shot up. He fumbled in his trouser pockets, withdrew an expensive looking black leather wallet and opened it. He produced a shiny black foil packet with a smile.

Kristina told herself again that this was wrong, but even before that thought had finished forming, she was reaching for the packet and tearing it open. He raised his hips as she set the condom on the blunt head of his thick cock and rolled it down, tugging it to reach the base of his length.

The moment she was done with it, Callum spread her legs, settled himself between them and eased into her.

He was gentler this time, moving with long slow strokes that threatened to set her on fire in a different way.

The heat of lust broke, turning into the heat of passion that Callum increased with each tender thrust of his body into hers.

Kristina kissed him, afraid of the slower tempo, falling a little more with each passing second. She had thought he had intended to push himself over the edge and into his orgasm by entering her, to take them both out of their minds again. If she had known he had intended to do this, she wouldn't have let him.

This felt too dangerous.

It felt too good.

She liked it too much.

He held her gently in his strong arms, his kisses lightening her insides, lifting her up and sending her soaring along with his slow deep thrusts. He groaned low in his throat and dipped one hand between them, brushing his fingers over her pert nub.

"Come with me, Kristina," he whispered against her lips and she breathed harder, each caress of her clit pushing her closer to the edge. "I want to feel it again."

Kristina couldn't deny him.

He thrust slowly into her and squeezed her nub at the same time, and she cried into his mouth, a sweep of hot tingles chasing outwards from the point where his cock filled her aching body, cascading along her thighs.

He groaned her name and plunged himself hard into her, his length throbbing again, quivering in rhythm with hers.

Callum kissed her softly, his body still locked with hers, and she melted into him, lost in how good it had felt to go slow with him.

Not good.

Dangerous.

She had no place doing such a thing with a vampire. Mindless passion and fucking was one thing. That meant nothing. That was what she had signed up for. He had changed everything and her heart said to run and not look back. This was more dangerous than remaining at her pack ever could have been.

She couldn't fall for a vampire.

He would only break her heart in the end.

"Kristina," he whispered against her throat between soft kisses. "Come to my hotel."

She froze, her entire body tensing. He kept kissing her, palms kneading the stiffness from her thighs and bottom, caressing her into submission.

"I have to leave Paris soon... just spend the next week here with me."

Kristina said nothing.

Her heart beat erratically in her throat.

Part of her said it was only a week. She could use it to wear out her craving for him and then he would be gone.

No hearts broken. No pain. Just a week of incredible sex.

The other part of her warned that it wouldn't just be sex. He would want to sleep with her in his arms.

Could she handle being held while she slept, protected from the world in the arms of a man she was intimate with?

He would want to feed her and take her out to dinner or nightclubs.

Could she handle being pampered when she had been alone so long, and dancing with him as she had tonight?

Even that had felt dangerously intimate. He would change the rules again and make love with her as he had just now and it would be game over.

He would break her heart.

Could she keep her head if that happened?

It would only take a tiny slip for her to give herself away to someone who knew her pack and then they would find her.

Could she handle being lonely when Callum left her?

Probably not.

There was a chance he would take her heart with him and she would never see him again.

Kristina was off him and dressing before she was aware of what she was doing.

Was she really going to run again?

She had fled her pack because she had been afraid of her alpha and his desire for her, and now she was fleeing Callum for the same reason.

Only this time it was different. She wanted him too.

She pulled her top on and fastened her jeans. The tall sides of her heeled black leather boots flapped downwards but she didn't care. She just had to get away and she would do it barefoot if it came to it.

Callum rose to his feet before her, removed the condom from his penis and tucked himself away. A wave of darkness crossed his expression.

"Callum, I..." she started but he pressed a single finger to her lips, silencing her, his expression lightening and turning his eyes soft with understanding.

"You don't have to answer right now. Just come to the Hotel George Cinq tomorrow night. I'll be waiting in the presidential suite." He replaced his fingers with his lips, pressing a gentle kiss to them that warmed her when it shouldn't have.

Before she could tell him that she wouldn't be coming, he was gone and the heavy black velvet curtain of the booth was falling back into place.

Kristina slumped onto the leather seat and stared at it for long seconds.

She raised her hand to her lips and touched them.

Hotel George Cinq. Presidential suite.

That sounded even more expensive than his fancy tailored clothes.

Just who was Callum?

There was one way of finding out the answer to that question.

But she still wasn't sure if she was brave enough to go through with it.

CHAPTER 4

Callum rubbed a fluffy white towel against his long wet hair and padded barefoot across the plush carpet of his hotel suite.

The gaudy decor was growing on him now but it still wasn't to his taste. He could never understand why luxury hotels felt the need to mix gold with dark blue and cream, and throw stripes into the mix too. It gave him a headache.

If Antoine had let him choose, he would have selected a different hotel, but the theatre had an account with this one and Antoine hadn't given him a choice about coming to Paris let alone the hotel where he would be staying.

Still, he couldn't really complain.

The room was more luxurious and decadent than his one at his family home in England and that was saying something. His family insisted on opulence.

Callum put it down to an attempt to gloss over the fact they were only elite vampires now and no longer the aristocrat purebloods their founding members had been.

Around a thousand years ago, the first human had been introduced into their family through turning and it had been all downhill from there. His father was a turned human, and so were his uncle and his grandmother.

Callum didn't care too much about the politics of it all but he did care about the fact that his kind were treated like second rate citizens by the aristocrats, as though the pure untainted vampire blood that ran in their veins gave them the right to look down on everyone.

He dropped the damp towel onto the back of a very expensive, very disgustingly upholstered couch, and tugged the one around his waist off.

He strode naked across the suite to the elegant wardrobe in the large bedroom and rifled through his clothes, the hangers squeaking as they moved along the rail.

Not all aristocrats were snobbish bastards though. Snow had proven himself vastly different to his brother Antoine just two months ago when he had stepped in and taken the rap for Javier's indiscretion with an owned human female.

Everyone had expected Snow to come back from meeting their rulers as a pretty jar of ashes but he had walked brazenly back into the theatre they ran together a week after leaving and said everything had been taken care of and that was that. Javier didn't need to stand trial for killing Lilah's owner and no one was going to be punished.

Antoine's relief had been palpable but if Callum had blinked at the wrong time he would have missed it.

Callum had always thought Snow was the coldest of the two aristocrats but it turned out he was wrong. Snow was merely icy most nights and Antoine was glacial all of the time.

If that was what it meant to be an aristocrat, then Callum was fine with being only an elite. He would rather have some humanity and dirty blood than a heart of ice and pure gold in his veins.

He glanced at the clock on the bedside table and frowned at the time. It was gone ten in the evening. The sun had set over two hours ago. She wasn't coming.

Callum pulled down a silver-grey shirt and slipped his arms into it. He fastened it as he looked over the trousers he had brought with him and chose a pair of slacks a few shades darker than his shirt. He considered coupling it all with his black silk tie and then dismissed it and undid the first two buttons of his shirt.

His gaze wandered to the windows and the night beyond. He wasn't sure what he would do if she didn't show. His pride said to let it be and not go out to the clubs in search of her. There was no need to look desperate. So, last night had been explosive and wild, and had felt so bloody good. That didn't mean he had to go chasing after her like an addict looking for another fix.

She was a werewolf.

That alone gave her reason not to show up, as did her reaction to him last night when he had wanted to bury his aching hungry cock in her again.

A condom.

He wasn't sure if a vampire could get a werewolf pregnant, and he was fairly certain that such precautions probably hadn't mattered at the time since he had already pumped his seed into her hot little body, but he was one hundred percent sure that the flip side to her reasoning was that he was a vampire.

Heaven forbid she let a vampire come in her.

What was she really afraid of? That someone would smell him on her, in her?

An image of the three built-like-brick-shithouses werewolves flashed across his mind.

Dread knotted his stomach.

He had been so fuzzy in the aftermath of his second coming that he had forgotten about the three men that he had taken her from.

What if she was with them and they smelt him on her? What if she wasn't with them?

It didn't matter either way.

If those three werewolves, especially the large one who had come close to biting a neck that he had earmarked as his and his alone, had smelt him all over her last night when she had emerged from the booth, she would have been in serious trouble.

And he had just left her there.

Alone.

Callum cursed and punched the wall next to the window, slamming his fist hard into the plaster. Pain ricocheted up his arm and down his spine. He ground his teeth and growled.

Fucking idiot.

How could he have left her like that?

He scrubbed a hand over his face. She probably wasn't coming because those three werewolves had waited for her to dare to leave the booth and had attacked her because of what he had done to her. Devil, they might have her now.

His heart clenched and he was halfway to the door before he realised what he was doing. He didn't stop when it dawned on him. He grabbed his black leather shoes, and his wallet off the side table, and kept walking. He would put his shoes on in the lift down to the lobby and would hail a taxi outside and head straight to the club.

When he reached it, he would bloody well sprint inside and demand that the vampire bartender told him where Kristina had gone after he had left.

There was a soft knock at his door.

Callum froze with his hand on the knob and reached out with his senses. The scent of werewolf came back to him, delicate and female, holding a faint sweet undertone that he recognised as strawberries. He peered through the peephole and his heart stopped.

Kristina stood on the other side, her slender frame swamped in a long black mac and her soft brown waves twisted into a knot at the back of her head. Her lips were glossy and red, the source of the strawberry scent on her. The knowledge that she would taste as sweet as her scent filled him with a need to tear the door open and kiss her. He drew a slow breath instead, calmed himself and then opened the door.

Her luminous eyes met his and he realised for the first time they were a beautiful hazel colour. She blinked slowly, long dark lashes shuttering her eyes, and then looked up at him.

"Not going to invite me in?" she said with false lightness.

It was no use pretending that she wasn't feeling on edge when he could sense the hint of fear spicing her blood.

Her smile faltered but held.

Callum resisted his need to pull her into his arms and smother her against his chest, to feel that she was safe and reassure himself that his eyes weren't playing cruel tricks on him. He ignored the reasons that popped into his head and told himself he was only feeling this way because he felt guilty about leaving her alone at the club last night.

"Come in." He stepped aside to allow her to enter.

Her hazel eyes widened so much he thought they would pop out of her head as she looked around the suite.

"This is amazing... they gave me the weirdest look downstairs when I asked where the presidential suite was." She turned back to him and smiled but it wavered and died on her lips, a look close to despair replacing it. "God... I feel like some high class hooker."

"They made you feel like a whore?" he growled and then cleared his throat and got hold of himself before he went down to reception and beat the crap out of them for it.

She smiled brightly. "No... they were surprised but nothing like that. I meant... coming here..."

The way she trailed off told him everything that she couldn't.

Christ.

Could he be any more of an idiot?

Not only had he left her alone last night to fend for herself when he should have escorted her out of the club and back to her place, ensuring she reached it safely, but his request that she spend the week with him had made her feel like a prostitute.

If the fact that she was a werewolf and he was a vampire wasn't reason enough for this relationship to fail before it even started, then his behaviour was.

He had treated her wrongly, had clearly left her feeling used and discarded, and practically commanded she come and fuck him for a week, and then forget it ever happened.

"Kristina," he said in a soft voice and held his hand out to her.

She remained in the middle of the area between the living room of the suite and the bedroom, her posture wary and the fear in her blood scent becoming something else, something worse. Hurt. She emitted the signals of a wounded creature.

Callum closed the door and crossed the room to her. He swept her into his arms and held her to his chest, one hand on the back of her head and his other arm wrapped around her shoulders. She sighed and he followed her, exhaling long and slow, searching for some solid ground when everything felt as though it was falling apart.

"I'm sorry," he whispered and she tensed and tried to break free of him.

The spark of panic was back and he thought he knew why.

She had panicked last night when he had slowed things down between them. She feared taking things to that level, just as he did. He hadn't meant to make love to her.

He had wanted it rough and wild like their first time, but the moment he had entered her, an intense need to feel every inch of her and absorb how good she felt moulded against him, her body responding so delightfully to his every caress and kiss, had seized him and he hadn't been strong enough to fight it. He smoothed the top of her hair, breathing slowly in an effort to convince her to do the same and relax.

"I royally fucked up last night. It shouldn't have ended like that." He caught her shoulders and drew her away from him.

She looked off to one side, towards the windows to her right, staring into the dark distance.

"It was what it was... let's not complicate things." Her eyes were dark when they met his, as cold and hard as steel. "It was just a bit of fun, right?"

She looked away again, gaze flitting over everything in the suite. Everything except him. It settled on the door.

"It was a mistake to come here. Last night was just a one time thing. This... I'm not strong enough to do this." Kristina broke free of his grasp, ducked under his outstretched arm, and stormed towards the door.

He caught her before she could reach it, clamping his hand down hard on her wrist. She stilled, her back to him, her eyes on his hand.

"What do you think this is?" he said, a little harder than he had wanted it to come out, and she whirled to face him.

"I don't know... but I know what you are," her tone turned accusatory and ended on a snarl. "You're just some aristocrat brat who thinks it would be great to have a werewolf at his beck and call for a week, fucking until he's sore... a grand tale to take back to his friends at the end of a fancy holiday and laugh over... what a joke, huh? A stupid dumb werewolf bitch on a leash, at her master's mercy, wagging her tale with joy whenever he chose to call her name and fuck her rabid. Well... it isn't going to happen. Get your hands off me."

She moved faster than he anticipated, knocking his hand aside before he could loosen his grip. His claws scraped over her flesh and he was so busy reeling from her verbal blows and the fact that they had triggered him to change that he didn't realise what was happening until the door slammed.

Crimson stained under his nails. He had cut her.

"Kristina." Callum curled his hand into a fist, pulled the door open and looked both ways along the hall. She was waiting for the lift far to his left, foot tapping as she clutched her wrist to her chest. "Kristina!"

She turned wild panicked eyes on him and pressed the call button again.

Once, twice, and then incessantly as he approached.

The lift doors pinged.

Callum reached them before she could enter, blocking her path and spreading his arms across the open doors.

"It isn't like that," he said and her hazel gaze met his.

Her grip on her wrist tightened and the scent of blood reached him, almost knocking him on his backside. He had never smelt anything like her. Potent, powerful, it had his head spinning from just the scent.

What would he feel like if he tasted it?

Callum shook his head to clear it and focused on his current predicament. There would be no blood if he couldn't make her see that she had got the wrong idea.

The doors behind him closed again and he relaxed.

"Why, because a vampire would never dare mention that he fucked a werewolf?" She practically spat the words at him.

He was starting to see why vampires had gone to war with werewolves several times in the past few centuries alone. He couldn't say a single word without her turning it against him.

"No." He kept his voice level, soothing, trying to decrease the elevated adrenaline in her blood.

The smell of it wasn't helping him keep his head.

He had to get her out of fight mode before the taut slender threads that held his urge to feed at bay snapped. He tried to touch her shoulder but she dipped it backwards out of his reach and glared at him. He sighed and lowered his hand to his side, resigning himself to not touching her even when he longed to hold her again and tell her that this had become more than just sex for him last night.

A couple rounded the end of the corridor and walked towards them. Humans.

"You know we can't do this here. Come back to the suite. Let me fix your wrist, pour you a drink, and explain myself."

She looked as though she would refuse and use the human couple as a shield so she could get on the lift without him daring to stop her.

Painful seconds ticked by, marked by the footsteps of the approaching humans.

Kristina nodded, placed her hands into the pockets of her coat so the couple didn't see the blood on her wrist, and started walking back towards his room.

Callum followed her, using the opportunity to get what he wanted to say straight in his head so he wouldn't mess it up. He opened the door for her and waited for her to step inside before following and closing it behind him.

Kristina sat on the striped couch in the living area.

Callum went to the small bar at the end of the room near the dining table, turned two crystal whisky glasses right way up and filled them to halfway with whatever expensive bottle he blindly grabbed.

He set one glass down in front of her on the polished wooden coffee table and clutched the other, pacing like a caged tiger, feeling more on edge than he had done in a long time. He cleared his throat, sniffed his drink and reconsidered it.

Alcohol played havoc with vampires.

What he really needed was a good swift shot of blood.

He sat down beside her on the blue and gold couch.

She didn't look at him.

"Firstly, I'm not an aristocrat. I come from an elite family."

She raised an eyebrow at him, her look unimpressed. It was the stupidest thing to open with but he didn't want her thinking that he was some heartless pureblood.

Surely she knew the difference between elite and aristocrat?

"I shouldn't have left you last night. Hell, I should have been a gentleman and then you wouldn't have come here feeling like you did. I can't undo the past. I fucked up. I admit it. I should have taken you home, kissed you, tucked you in and made sure you were safe. The werewolves didn't bother you did they?" He tilted his head so he could see into her eyes.

She lowered them further and gave an almost imperceptible nod.

"Christ... Kristina... they didn't hurt you did they?"

Her expression turned to one of shock and her gaze leapt up to his. "What do you care if they did?"

"I care." Callum risked brushing his knuckles down her cheek and held her gaze, his own steady and unwavering. "I'd kill the bastards if they laid one finger on you."

Her eyes shot wide. "You would kill three strong members of a local pack? The rest would come after you. You'd probably trigger the next war between our species. Have you lost your mind?"

Callum smiled. "I think I have. Ever since that dance, I can't think straight when you're around me. I do the opposite of everything I know I should be doing. I think I should take you home and I leave you in the club alone instead. I think I should ask you if you'd like to spend some time with me and see how things go and I demand you come to my hotel and spend my final week in Paris in my bed."

She continued to stare at him in silence.

He sighed again.

"I never meant to make you feel like a whore. Give me another chance and I'll say things right this time." Callum took hold of her hand and she didn't pull away. She tilted her knees towards him and lifted her eyes to his, and he couldn't miss the expectant look in them. "I have a week left in Paris, and last night was incredible, and I don't want it to be a 'one time thing', as you put it. It went beyond just a little fun for me... and I can't stop thinking about you. I know the odds are against us... but I can't ignore how good it felt to be with you and I want to feel that again. I want to see if this thing between us is more than fleeting... Yes, I'm aware how crazy that sounds and I'll point you back to my earlier statement. I have lost my mind. I lost it the moment I kissed you—and the smell of your blood is driving me crazy too."

She looked down at her bleeding wrist, turning it upwards to reveal the three ragged red lines scoring her pale skin. He was thankful that the cuts were shallow, more like scratches, and he hadn't reached any veins.

He hadn't meant to end on talking about her blood. A bolt of panic had forced his mind to leap to another subject when the words had lined up on his tongue and he had found them to be shocking. If they shocked him then they would send her running and he didn't want that.

He wanted her to stay right here.

With him.

Callum stared into her eyes, waiting to hear her answer, aware of the knot in his chest and what it meant.

CHAPTER 5

Kristina picked up her glass of whisky, sipped it demurely, as though she was enjoying keeping him teetering on the edge, desperate to hear whether she was going to stay, and then set it down on her knee. She looked right into his eyes, her hazel ones no longer cold or dark, and stared into them for the longest time.

Callum was close to demanding an answer by the time she finally spoke.

"You're serious about this?" She took another sip of whisky. Did she need it to boost her courage? If it would do the same for him rather than going straight to his head, knocking him flat and leaving him needing more blood than usual, he would be downing the two fingers he had poured for himself. "You know whatever friends you have back where you came from would tear you a new one if they found out about me."

He was well aware of that. Antoine would do more than tear him a new one.

Javier's murder of Lilah's master and consequent claiming and turning of her had left their leader in a foul mood and with a lot on his plate. It had taken a monumental amount of effort on the aristocrat's part to smooth things over with the pureblood community and convince them to continue pledging their money to and attending the performances at Vampirerotique.

If word reached Antoine that Callum had been sleeping with what most vampires saw as the enemy, he would have his head, after he had made him suffer first.

And yet Callum still found himself opening his mouth and saying, "I've never been more serious... and I don't care what people think. I want you, and that is all that matters to me."

She shook her head, an incredulous look in her eyes, and set her whisky glass down on the coffee table.

"Just as long as you're aware of what we're doing here." Her gaze met his again.

"Are you?" he countered and she blinked, dropped her eyes back to the glass and shrugged.

"I gave up caring about things a long time ago, and I don't have any friends. In fact... it could only be a good thing for me if word that I had slept with a vampire filtered down the vine to my pack."

Callum had to wonder why that was. Her pack would likely disown her and never associate with her again. Was that something she wanted? Come to think of it. She was definitely British like he was, and based on the fact that no one seemed familiar with her in the clubs, she was new to Paris.

"Where is your pack based?" he said and the warmth in her eyes evaporated in an instant, turning cold as her guard went up and shut him out.

"No questions," she snapped and stood. "If we're going to do this, you don't go probing into my personal life and I don't go asking about yours. Got it?"

The pack was definitely a sour subject for her. Her reaction only increased his curiosity about it. Had she parted with them on bad terms? His eyebrows rose. Was she on the run? She had panicked and he had sensed fear in her the whole time she had been with the werewolf last night.

Afraid that the man would know her pack from her scent and contact them?

He wanted to ask about it but held his tongue. The fire now blazing in her eyes warned him not to even dare to disagree with her. She would be out of the door again if he did, and he didn't want that. As much as he wanted to know her past, he wanted her more fiercely.

Callum nodded.

He would wait until her guard was down and then do a little digging. It wasn't just her safety at risk. If she was running from her pack and they were after her, he could end up caught in the crossfire.

She had said that he would start a war by killing the three werewolves from last night.

She would start one herself if her pack discovered she had chosen a vampire over her own kind. They would want vengeance. His death would be the start of another bloodbath between vampires and werewolves.

"Fine." Callum rose to his feet. He brushed the backs of his fingers across her cheek and her armour fell away again, lowering to reveal a touch of warmth in her eyes that he was growing to like seeing. "I won't ask why you're running."

A flicker of steel in her gaze and the twitch of her body as she tensed told him that he had presumed right. She was on the run from her pack. Why?

Kristina stepped up to him and rested her hands on his chest.

Her fingertips caressed him through the silky grey material, teasing and pushing the thought out of his mind as his body responded to her touch. He slid his hand around the nape of her neck and tipped her head back so her eyes met his.

The rosy gloss on her lips still tempted him with its scent but it was the lingering fragrance of her blood in the air that had saliva pooling in his mouth and his fangs itching to taste her.

He clamped down on the desire, forcing it deep inside him and keeping it there.

She was already on edge as it was.

Transforming in front of her again would probably send her dashing for the door. As much as he desired her, as fiercely as his hunger for her rode him, he would keep himself under control.

He wouldn't bite her until she asked.

She hesitated and so did he. The hunger that had given him confidence last night was little more than a fizzling ember, reduced to ashes by everything that had passed between them in the past half an hour. He wasn't sure what to do to bring it back or how to move past this awkward silence. He wanted to kiss her again, craved the flavour of her on his tongue, but wasn't sure if she wanted it too.

"This is stupid," she muttered under her breath, leapt up and wrapped her legs around his hips and her arms around his shoulders.

It caught him off balance and sent him tripping backwards across the room, desperately clutching her bottom to support her. He hit the door hard, the brass knob jabbing him in the back and pushing the air from his lungs in a harsh grunt.

She beamed at him. "Wow... I had thought you would have been able to handle that."

"A little warning wouldn't go amiss," he grumbled and straightened his back, grimacing as the area that had collided with the door knob throbbed and ached.

"Clearly you're not as strong as I thought you were." She grinned.

Callum stared at her, feeling as though she had mentally cast him out of the role of male vampire and onto the reject pile labelled 'human'.

Not as strong as she thought?

Well. If she had thought to challenge his masculinity, she had chosen the perfect words for it, and he would respond with the perfect counter argument.

Still holding her, he strode across the room, tossed her onto the bed, and before she had stopped bouncing in the middle of it, was on her. His fingers clamped tightly around her wrists and pinned them hard to the soft striped dark blue and gold covers. Her smile fell away and her pupils dilated when he growled down at her, his hips against hers, holding her immobile and powerless beneath him.

Her fingers flexed and she struggled, a wicked glint in her eyes commanding him to stop her.

Vixen.

She liked it.

He shifted his grip, interlocked their fingers, and pressed her hands down harder, until his muscles tensed, his body went taut, and the urge to snarl tore through him. The scent of her arousal hit him hard. The black chasms of her pupils ate the colour in her irises, confirming her hunger.

Callum snarled and kissed her, forcing her mouth open with his tongue. She moaned and writhed against him, her hands pushing up into his. She almost managed to get the back of her hands off the quilt.

Almost.

He pressed more of his weight onto her slender hands, stopping her before she managed it, and she groaned and kissed him harder, her teeth clashing with his as their mouths met in short desperate bursts. He wanted to touch her, slide his hands over her supple body and reacquaint himself with her breasts, stomach and groin, but that meant surrendering his grip on her.

He was sure the moment he did such a thing, she would have him flat on his back, pinned beneath her, showing him he wasn't in control and that she could match his strength.

She couldn't.

Werewolves were weaker than vampires, and he was fairly certain that he was much older than her too.

"Callum," she breathed into his mouth and he dropped his lips to her throat, kissing and licking, driven by the sound of his name falling so huskily from her lips.

He wanted to hear her scream it, needed to be aware of her climax and feel the pleasure rippling through her, knowing that he had given it to her.

He nipped her collarbone with his blunt teeth and then snarled when he reached the black mac she still wore. He wanted it off her.

Kristina didn't move when he sat back and released her hands. She laid on the bed beneath him, panting breathlessly, her breasts heaving delightfully. He made fast work of the belt on her coat and then pulled it open.

His breath stuttered.

Hell.

He wanted to devour her now.

She looked too delicious in the little dark red leather corset and short pleated black skirt. If he had known she was wearing this beneath her plain boring mac, he probably wouldn't have let her out of the suite the first time. He probably wouldn't have given her a chance to lash out at him. He would have been worshipping her with kisses the moment he had set eyes on her and plunging himself into her warm sheath just a heartbeat later.

"Christ... fuck me," he whispered, at a loss as to what to do next. He wasn't sure where to start.

"Okay." She grabbed his shoulder and flipped him onto his back on the bed.

He sank into it, not putting up a fight as she removed her mac and tossed it onto the bed beside her.

The vision of her astride him, her smooth creamy thighs tight against his hips, the short black skirt that barely covered her crotch, and the wicked strapless leather corset that squashed her breasts into cleavage that took his breath away, rendered him dumb.

She wriggled her hips against him and he groaned at the feel of her heat seeping through his dark grey trousers and the exquisite friction of her pussy rubbing along his rigid cock.

Callum clutched her hips, breathing hard and struggling to form words.

A compliment would do.

He tried one but it came out garbled because she chose that moment to lean over him and blind him with the sight of her full breasts verging on spilling out of her corset. It was a miracle they stayed in.

He wished they hadn't.

He wanted to swirl his tongue around each rosy button in turn and suckle them until she moaned for more.

"Did you say something?" She frowned at him and ran her hands over his chest, heading for the buttons of his silver shirt.

She undid them slowly, her fingers brushing his skin as she popped each one and parted his shirt a little. When she had undone the final button, she eased the two sides apart to reveal his torso.

He swallowed and forced a single word out. "Beautiful."

She ran an appraising glance over him and smiled. "Funny... I was just thinking the same thing."

He groaned and bucked at the first touch of her hot mouth on his flesh. She trailed wet kisses over his chest, pausing to circle his left nipple with her tongue, and down to his stomach. She growled, the sound rumbling low in her throat, and his cock throbbed in response.

He had never been with a woman who growled like he did when excited and aroused. It made him think of her biting him and he was surprised by how much he welcomed the thought.

Callum tipped his head back into the soft duvet, groaning as she lightly bit near his navel. He clutched the bedclothes, twisting them into his fists, and she giggled.

"You looked delicious enough when you weren't tense," she murmured in a heated way and lavished his stomach with kisses, licking and nipping at him. "Damn, you look irresistible now. I might have to eat you."

Hell.

He rolled his eyes closed and groaned again, every muscle going taut as she raked her nails over his chest, catching his nipples, and down his stomach to his belt. His breathing hitched with the tug of her hands on his belt and he exhaled all the air in his lungs as the sound of his zipper sliding down filled the silent room.

"Mmm," she moaned and stroked his hard length through his boxers.

He bucked against her palm, unable to control himself.

She drove that ability away. Shattered all thought and left him with only instinct. His hips pumped, rubbing his hungry cock against her hand, leaving him aching for flesh-to-flesh contact between them.

"Let's see if you're as damn beautiful as I remember."

Callum bit his lower lip, her words swimming in his hazy mind, slowly working themselves into the right order to form her sentence.

She thought his cock was beautiful?

He was about to pursue an answer to that question when she shuffled his boxers down over his hips and ran her tongue along the length of his erection, from root to tip, shattering his ability to think again. He groaned instead, fingers tightening against the duvet.

The first swirl of her soft pink tongue around the head of his cock sent his head spinning and he grunted.

She made a little noise of pleasure, a tiny murmur that died as she took him into her mouth. The wet slide of her tongue down the underside of his erection and the slight scrape of her teeth along the top, sent a shiver of tingles tripping through him. He grunted again, aware that he was starting to sound like some sort of animal but unable to muster enough care to stop.

She made him into an animal.

Each warm slide of her mouth down his cock, each brush of the back of her throat over the sensitive head, each press of her tongue against the underside as she rose off him, and each torturous swirl around the blunt head had his moans turning into snarls and his snarls becoming growls. His balls tightened and she chose that moment to cup them in her palm and roll them, increasing the tension at the base of his cock.

She moaned and the sound of it joining his constant snarls and growls of bliss, the thought that she took pleasure from doing this to him, from making him feel so good that he was burning up inside, couldn't stop himself from thrusting shallowly into her mouth as he sought his orgasm, only turned him on even more.

She squeezed his balls, stroked the area just below them, and then rubbed it as she sucked him harder.

Callum's climax came upon him like a tidal wave, obliterating all conscious thought and leaving him with only intense feelings.

He pressed his hips up, thrusting his cock into her mouth, and cried her name as he came.

Fire blazed through his veins and limbs, sending them quaking, stealing his breath and almost stopping his heart. He screwed his face up, trembling all over, struggling to catch his breath as she licked and sucked him, her breathy little moans adding to the ecstasy carrying him away.

He couldn't move.

His muscles were slack and weak, bones limp and useless. He lay on the bed beneath her, eyes closed, heart beating erratically, breathless.

Christ, if he hadn't wanted to let her go before, he really didn't want to let her go now. He had never experienced something so intense and mind-blowing, not in all his five hundred plus years.

"Good?" she said with an obvious giggle in her voice. She was teasing him. She knew it was good, was well aware of the fact she had reduced him to a quivering mess.

She crawled up the length of him and after several seconds he managed to get his heavy eyelids up and looked into her eyes.

"You're smiling like a crazy person." She giggled again, her hazel eyes full of light and warmth.

She was beautiful, so full of life and so intoxicating.

She sparkled with it, bright and blinding, completely different to how she had been around other men.

There had always been wariness in her eyes then. It had even been there when she had been with him at the club.

It was gone now.

Was this sudden change in her because she felt safe with him?

Had she been scared the whole time she had been out in the world?

He wanted to make her feel this way all the time. He wanted to ride in on a white steed and play her knight in shining armour so she would never be scared again. His chest heated, heart steadying as he realised and admitted that the knot that he had felt in it before was more than fleeting.

He really was falling for her.

He lifted his arm, brushed his knuckles across her cheek and then opened his hand and cupped her face, resting his fingertips close to her ear.

Her look changed instantly, a cautious edge entering her eyes, stealing some of the light from their hazel depths.

Callum wanted to tell her to stop running away from him whenever he tried to show her the slightest emotion beyond simple lust and desire, but he knew that it would only make her bolt.

She trembled beneath his touch and he could feel the fear rising in her again.

Would she run if he told her that she didn't need to fear him and that he wouldn't hurt her?

Of course she would.

She wasn't ready to hear such things from him.

"I think you broke me," he whispered and her smile returned, the hint of fear in her scent fading.

He lowered his hand from her face, caught her right wrist, and brought it away from his chest. He frowned at the scratches across it.

"I didn't mean to hurt you." He glanced up at her to find her staring at her wrist, her eyes round and distant.

She didn't tense or pull away when he inhaled slowly to catch the scent of her blood. It was still intoxicating, the undertones of sweetness and spice sparking hunger inside him. He was sure she would taste like nothing he had ever experienced before. He had smelt werewolf blood in the past and it hadn't been like hers. It had been flat and dull, as uninteresting as most vampires' blood.

What made hers so different?

Kristina stilled when he drew her hand towards him and reached out with his tongue, his eyes half closing as he came close to touching the scratches. She withdrew her hand and clucked her tongue.

"No bloodplay." She tortured him by licking her own wrist, stealing what he had wanted to be his, and sat up astride him. Her fingers glided up his stomach to his chest and then down his arms to his wrists. She took hold of his hands and raised them, placing them on her hips and sliding them up to her breasts. "You're not shaking anymore."

He focused on his body and noted that she was right. He had stopped trembling the moment she had sat back on him, nestling his soft cock against her groin. The feel of her heat on him, their bodies separated by only her underwear, had pushed him through the haze of one orgasm into the search for his next.

She smiled when his penis twitched, stirring at the thought of being inside her this time.

"You vampires certainly do have the stamina everyone says you do," she said and he frowned at her.

When had she closed herself off again?

She spoke about him as though they were strangers fucking for fun and he was just a vampire and she just a werewolf.

They weren't Callum and Kristina.

Had she seen in his eyes what he had wanted to say, that he had moved past this being about nothing more than satisfying urges and cravings, and this was her reaction to it?

She hesitated, crimson turning her cheeks rosy, and toyed with his nipples, staring at them. She obviously had acute senses because she had picked up on the barest threads of his emotions and right now she was feeling his anger.

"Kristina," he said, unwilling to let her pretend that this meant nothing.

He would force her to use his name if he had to. He wouldn't stop using hers. He could be cruel too, could call her werewolf or female, could place that barrier between them.

How would she like that? Would it hurt her as much as her doing the same hurt him?

He pulled her down to him and kissed her, deliberately slowly, forcing her to acknowledge that this could be something more than just a moment of madness if she wanted it to be and could accept him in her life. She struggled at first, trying to roughen the kiss and turn it passionate.

He didn't let her.

Her version of passion wasn't what he wanted this to be about. He wanted it to be about passion that meant something, that came from the heart and soul, not the sex glands.

Kristina relaxed into him, her kisses slowing to match his, her lips a bare caress that left his tingling and lightened his insides. He wrapped his arms around her, unwilling to let her go before he was done with her, holding her gently to instil a sense of safety inside her again. He wanted the Kristina who had looked at him so softly with bright warm eyes back.

"Callum," she whispered against his mouth, a note of desire in her tone, and swept her tongue over his lower lip, igniting sparks that exploded over his skin and down his spine. He groaned and tried to kiss her but she held herself out of his reach, teasing him with soft licks over his lips that cranked him tighter with each one. "I want you."

Callum raised his hips into hers, pushing his hardening cock against her groin to show her that he wanted her too. She wasn't alone in this. If she would only accept that, he was sure that she would feel less on edge about what they were doing and would realise that he wasn't out to hurt her.

Hell. At this rate, it would end with him being the one hurt by her.

Since leaving her last night, he had told himself close to a thousand times not to go down this route and to just let things happen and see where it took them.

He had warned himself not to get attached or read into things. It was impossible after all. He could warn himself all he wanted, could point out the dangers of becoming emotionally attached to a werewolf, but none of it was stopping him from wanting more from her.

He groaned low in his throat as she rose to her feet, standing with her boots on either side of his hips, and wriggled her black knickers down her thighs. She lifted each foot off the bed in turn, pulling her knickers over them, and then tossed them down at him.

Callum gathered them into his fist and held her gaze as he brought them to his nose and inhaled the scent of her arousal. His cock leapt, growing harder at the thought that he made her wet and hungry.

She wanted him.

Kristina lowered herself again, her bare thighs warm against his sides, and then shuffled backwards, seating herself over his knees. She grabbed her mac and rifled in the pockets, and pulled out a strip of condoms. She had come prepared this time. He was still fairly certain that he couldn't impregnate her but he held his tongue, letting her have her way. Anything to get back inside her.

She pulled his trousers and boxers down to his knees, tore open the packet, and rolled the condom down onto his cock. It pulsed as he stared down at her skirt and then took in her outfit again, realising that she intended to have sex with him while still wearing it.

He wasn't going to complain.

She looked incredibly sexy in the tight corset and short skirt, and he liked the thought of her remaining in it a while longer and riding him. It added a naughty edge to everything. He had never been into the whole dressing up thing, but the thought of her in a dirty maid's outfit or dressed as a dominatrix took on a certain appeal as she moved up his body.

Kristina rose off him, wrapped her hot little hand around his cock, and nudged the tip of him inside her liquid heat.

He watched her face, mesmerised by the visible pleasure she took from the feel of his cock sliding slowly into her tight sheath and the breathless moan that accompanied it from the moment he entered her to the point where he was fully inside.

She settled on him, her body tightly gloving him and encasing him in fiery heat. He almost begged her not to move, to stay right there and let him just feel what it was like to be inside her, joined as one with such a beautiful woman.

Her hands pressed into his stomach and then skimmed up to his ribs and chest, her eyes locked on his, her body clenching him but unmoving, as though she had felt his desire and was letting him have his way. She brushed her fingers down his arms, caught his hands and pressed her palms to his.

Callum interlinked their fingers and held her hands as she started to move on him, slow long thrusts that soon had her closing her eyes and tipping her head back.

He stared at her, entranced, watching the pleasure rippling across her face as she flickered between frowning and sighing. The soft black material of her skirt caressed his lower stomach and thighs. The scent of her desire filled the room, joining with his, swirling together into one tantalising fragrance.

Her thrusts slowly built in speed, turning harder but still remaining more gentle than he had thought she would be. The pace of her movements on him matched his pace during their second time last night.

Too slow to be lust.

Too slow not to mean something.

She gasped, her hands squeezing his, and rode him. The exquisite feel of her hot sheath encasing him, pulling at him, clenching him, and the warm trickle of her juices down his cock, all of it was blissful and arousing, but it was the pleasure on her face, her slow tempo, and the way she opened her eyes and locked them on his, revealing a myriad of feelings in their hazel orbs that went beyond mere desire, that left him breathless again. It was the most erotic thing he had ever seen.

Chains, whips, naughty outfits, none of it could hold a candle to how the slow shift of her body against his and the emotions warming her eyes made him feel. It felt so intimate. He felt so connected to her, not just physically through the point where his body entered hers, but emotionally through their eyes.

Callum stared into hers, lost and mesmerised, feeling them sweep him away and seeing that sensation mirrored in her.

She barely blinked as she looked deep into his eyes and he into hers, their bodies moving as one, hers sliding sensually up and down his cock.

Her heart beat steadily in his mind, his coming to match it, so they joined too. Her lips parted and so did his, the feelings flooding him making him feel as though he was drowning and gasping for air.

The room faded, leaving only her on his senses—her pulse, her soft puffs, her little moans of pleasure that he echoed, her sweet scent filling his mind as his body filled hers.

Kristina.

He felt as though he was falling, the world dropping away beneath him, plunging deep into unfamiliar territory. It scared him but her grip on him soothed away the fear and the soft warmth in her eyes anchored him to her, until he felt as though they were falling together.

Did she feel it too?

Her eyelids fell to half mast and she gasped. "Callum."

Her fingers pressed into the back of his hands and she jerked against him, her body quaking around his as her thrusts faltered. He took over, driving his cock into her as she started to lean into his hands, her hot breath skating over his stomach and chest.

She moaned with each deep plunge of his cock and the feel of her body clenching and releasing him, the hot rush of her orgasm, pushed him over the edge with her.

"Kristina," he breathed and bucked his hips up hard, burying himself deep into her body as he came. The fierce wave that rushed through him sent his head spinning.

He was vaguely aware of her lips on his wrist, the warm press of her tongue, and then fire that exploded through him. A second orgasm rocked him to the core and the world went dark.

"Callum... Cal... lum... Cal... can you hear me?"

He frowned and knocked aside the annoying object tapping his cheek like a bloody woodpecker on acid. It didn't go away. If anything, it became more frantic.

"Cal? Callum... you're scaring me now... wake up, you bloody vampire... you're stronger than this." Firm hands grabbed his shoulders and rattled him.

He smacked them away, snarled, and shot one hand out at his attacker. He locked it tight around whatever it hit first and squeezed.

"Cal... lum." The irritating voice sounded more distant, turning tighter and strained as he increased the pressure of his grip. "You're... hurting... me..."

Hurting?

Callum's eyes shot open and instantly closed against the brightness that assaulted him. His head spun until he felt on the verge of vomiting.

Someone grabbed his wrist, tugging at it.

He slowly rolled his eyes open again.

Kristina's hands were locked tightly around his wrist.

Trying to pull his hand away from her throat.

Tears lined her dark lashes and fear shone in her irises.

Callum sat up fast, sending his head spinning violently, and crashed back onto the bed again, his hand slipping from her throat. He closed his eyes and groaned.

What had happened?

He remembered how incredible it had felt making love to Kristina and then it all went hazy.

"Are you alright?" The hoarseness of her voice stabbed him deep in the gut.

He had said he wouldn't hurt her but he had. It had been an instinctive reaction, which meant something bad had happened to him. All vampires reacted on instinct when they felt they were in danger or were hurt so badly that they lost their more human side because of the pain.

"What happened?" he ground the words out and the world slowly stopped spinning around him.

He risked opening his eyes again and found Kristina leaning over him, one hand on her bruised throat and the other stroking his cheek.

"You blacked out," she whispered almost apologetically. "You don't remember?"

He shook his head and she looked as though she didn't want to bring up why he had passed out. She bit her lip, hesitated, and then blushed.

"I got a little carried away... and I, uh, well..." She glanced down at his left hand.

Callum frowned.

It was aching.

Now that he noticed it, he recalled that she had kissed his wrist and his entire body had come alive, burning so fiercely that he had climaxed again.

He slowly raised his left hand and slid his gaze across to it.

Ragged red marks formed a rough broken circle on the point just below his wrist.

He blinked.

"I... it won't happen again... I didn't realise that you were going to pass out or anything like that. I just... I know what I said earlier... but the urge struck me and I sort of followed through without thinking." Her words were a blur after that, a running apology that collided into nothing more than noise in his aching head.

She had bitten him.

He raised his eyebrows and stared blankly at the bloodstained wound.

The first release when they had felt so close and connected had been incredible enough. The second had come upon him without warning, fierce and violent, intense.

Because of her bite?

He looked back into her eyes.

"Are you sure you're alright?" She touched his cheek, her eyebrows high on her forehead, concern filling her eyes. "You look a little out of it still."

"Did you feel it too?" he said and her cheeks blazed, turning her whole face crimson this time.

She went to glance away but then stopped herself and nodded. The awkward edge to her expression became nerves and her fingers trembled against his face.

"Did you pass out too?" he whispered and her eyes widened. It was all the answer he needed. "Why?"

Kristina shrugged but he saw straight through it. She knew why but she wasn't going to mention it.

It was possible that they had both overloaded when she had bitten him.

Vampires were capable of blacking out when bitten. There was nothing quite like the feel of someone sinking their fangs into your flesh at the right moment during sex. He hadn't thought werewolves would share such a kink though.

Was that all it was?

The look in her eyes said not to press her for an answer. She climbed off him, sat on the bed with her legs tucked to one side, and traced patterns on the duvet.

Callum slowly pushed himself up onto his elbows. The condom was gone. How long had he been out?

He glanced at the clock on the bedside table. It was close to five A.M., which meant he must have been out cold for over five hours. It had felt like only a moment.

He rose from the bed, stripped off his trousers and underwear, and then held his hand out to her. She looked at it as though it was going to bite her.

"I didn't mean to hurt you." He pressed one knee into the mattress and brushed his knuckles across her throat. It still bore the impression of his fingers. How close had he been to strangling her? "It was instinct. Surely werewolves experience something similar when disorientated or injured?"

Her gaze zipped to the bed again. He hadn't meant to imply that she had injured him. He wasn't angry about what she had done. The pleasure of it had just been too much and he hadn't been able to take it.

"Kristina, I'm not going to hurt you... and I know you didn't mean to hurt me. It was just the heat of the moment. I felt the urge to bite you too... you were just beyond my reach." He cupped her cheek and brought her head around so she was facing him again, her eyes on his.

The shyness in them made him smile. She was worrying and not because she feared his anger. For a werewolf who tried so hard to keep her distance, she was doing a terrible job of it right now. Her eyes were so open, reflecting feelings that reassured him that it wouldn't be hard to convince her that something was happening between them. It also reassured him that she didn't find the idea of him biting her repulsive.

"If you want to bite me again, I would like that. Although, perhaps, not during sex. If you want me to bite you, we can do that too. We can do whatever you're comfortable with. Does that sound alright with you?"

She surprised him by nodding, slipping her hand into his, and coming to stand before him.

"Now, it's almost dawn." Callum wrapped his free arm around her waist and ran his fingers down the lacing at the back of her corset. "As regrettable as it is to get you out of this sexy little number... it has to come off. I want to sleep next to you."

He shifted his hand lower, to her skirt, and raised it. Her bottom was soft as feathers beneath his fingers and she bit her lip and pressed her hands into his bare chest. He let her go. If they kept on like this, the sun would have long risen before he finally fell asleep with her tucked against him.

Her wide pupils lured him in.

Callum heaved a sigh.

Undressing her was going to play havoc with his libido anyway. They would just have to sleep in late.

He grabbed her backside and raised her up his body. She wrapped her legs around his waist, looped her arms around his neck, and kissed him.

Callum fell onto the bed with her beneath him and set about making her cry his name all over again.

CHAPTER 6

Kristina woke slowly, sated and sleepy, the duvet and the naked vampire wrapped around her combining to make the perfect temperature for snoozing the night away.

Callum's bare front moulded against her back, his right arm heavy over her waist, hand cupping her right breast, anchoring her to him. Her own right hand was hooked behind her, holding his firm backside. His cool breath puffed against her throat, slow and steady, and he felt as bone tired on her senses as she did.

In her one hundred and twelve years of life, she had never felt so safe, not even as a youngling in her mother's arms.

The way Callum held her pressed so close to him so there wasn't a millimetre where their bodies didn't touch and the sleepy growls that accompanied any shift of his body against hers or tightening of his grip, made her feel so protected. She was sure that if anyone came for her here and right now that he would instantly snap awake and fend them off.

But how long could this fairytale last?

He had already said that he would leave Paris in a week.

Everything else he said came rushing into her mind like a dam had broken and flooded it, driving out the comfort of sleeping in his arms. He had made out as though he felt things were already more than just a fling between them to him and had said some fairly pretty words that most women would have been flattered to hear.

God, they had flattered her. She had almost gone along with him and let her guard drop, but then she had got the better of herself.

And then he had proven that he could see straight through her.

He knew she was on the run from her pack.

He had seen through her later too, when they had been screwing. Making love. She couldn't even bring herself to lie about it and pretend it had just been sex. That had been more than just sex, and more than making love. It had been intense, consuming, and incredible.

But the emotional ties that had formed between them scared her.

They left her vulnerable and tore at her.

When she had come around to find that he had passed out too, she had wanted to run and not look back. It wasn't just the bite that had sent them both over the edge. It was their blood combining. She had drunk deeply in the short time before she had slipped into unconsciousness, greedily sucking down his rich blood.

How much of it was still in her, tying them together?

She had fled her alpha because he had learned that she was ripe for mating and wanted to sire a child with her and tie her to him.

Her mother had told her about mating before she had passed away. Compatible mates often experienced things more intensely, and highly compatible ones even more so, to the point where both the male and the female involved often passed out during a mutual climax when she was receptive and ready to bear a cub.

Her mother had never mentioned anything about a blood exchange though. Kristina fiercely held onto that, using it to ward off her fear. They had passed out because the combination of sex and blood had proven too much for both of them.

That was all it had been.

She wouldn't take his blood again during sex, or let him take hers, and that would prove that she was right.

They had been intimate a number of times without either of them blacking out. It was just the involvement of blood.

A vampire couldn't be a mate to a werewolf.

It wasn't genetically possible.

Werewolves had broken away from their human ancestors millennia ago. Vampires were a completely different race, bearing only a physical resemblance to a human.

A heavy feeling settled in her stomach.

She stared at the far wall in the cream bedroom until it swam out of focus.

Callum was an elite.

Didn't that mean he had human blood in his family?

She had never heard of a vampire impregnating a werewolf, or vice versa, but what about a human?

He stirred behind her, sighing against her throat, and crushed her to his chest.

Her stomach grumbled in response to the squeeze.

"You sound hungry," he murmured and kissed the nape of her neck. It tickled and she wriggled and then froze when she felt the press of his cock against her backside.

She was hungry, and encouraging him to get a hard-on wasn't going to get her fed.

"You want breakfast?" He snuggled closer to her, as though he was trying to convince her to say no and stay in bed with him.

"It's gone five in the afternoon. I don't think they serve breakfast at this time."

He chuckled, pushed himself up on one elbow behind her and dropped a tender kiss on her shoulder. She turned her head to look up at him.

Long strands of his black hair had fallen out of his ponytail and brushed his cheek.

She had never been one for long hair but she didn't mind it on him, although if she had her way she would convince him to cut it into a shorter wilder style that would suit his handsome face so much better.

Still, he looked sexy as hell all rumpled from sleep, his green eyes soft and warm.

He pressed his lips to her shoulder, looking up at her through his lashes, his expression sweet and boyish.

"Look around you. You're in the presidential suite in an obscenely expensive hotel. I think you can order whatever you like and they would rush to get it for you."

"Even blood?" she said and his expression darkened.

"Unfortunately not." He swept his lips over her shoulder and nestled his crotch against her bottom. "That is something we have to go out and collect ourselves. Are you hungry for blood?"

She shook her head. "You?"

Kristina feared he would say yes. The few mouthfuls she had stolen from him last night had satisfied that side of her hunger but she was sure that it would have left him with a need to feed and replenish what she had taken.

"I'm fine for now. Elite vampires don't need as much blood as our aristocrat brethren."

Because of the human element in their DNA?

She wanted to say it aloud but wasn't brave enough to hear him confirm that he was part human like she was.

"So, do you want to eat or not?" He reached over her, grabbed the phone from the bedside table, and settled back into bed behind her.

Kristina rolled to face him, pressing half of her body into his as he lay on his back, patiently holding the phone with his finger hovering over the button that would put him through to room service. She was hungry but she was also afraid he was going to think she was a pig when she started rattling off the growing list of food she wanted.

"Well?" His eyebrows rose.

"You really can't eat anything?"

"Not a sausage," he said with a smile and her mouth watered at the thought of sausages. "But don't let that stop you. I'll order your food, wait for it to arrive, and then shower while you're eating if you don't want an audience."

She cursed him for seeing straight through her again.

"Okay." She blew out her breath and he punched the number and brought the phone to his ear.

"This is the presidential suite. We would like to order some food," he said into the receiver and then looked at her.

Kristina rattled off everything she had a hankering for and listened to him repeat it, his emerald eyes growing wider and wider with each item. Bacon. Scrambled eggs. Toast. Marmalade. Croissants. Sausages. Fried tomatoes. Sautéed potatoes. Pancakes. Waffles. Strawberries. Chocolate sauce. Orange juice.

She was shocked herself when her list continued. Every time she said one thing, another two popped into her mind and she wanted to eat them too.

"Did you get all that?" Callum said to the person on the other end of the phone when she was done, his eyebrows still glued to his hairline.

She presumed the person responded positively because he ended the call and let the phone fall onto the bed. He stared at her.

"You really are hungry. I suppose you didn't eat lunch or dinner last night."

Yeah. That was her excuse and she was sticking to it. She hadn't eaten in almost two days in fact, not since her money had started to run low.

Callum grinned, grabbed her and rolled on top of her as he kissed her. The urgent sweep of his lips over hers, the teasing strokes of his tongue, pushed her embarrassment away and she melted into the bed beneath him, enjoying the warmth of the duvet and the feel of their naked bodies tangled together.

She wrapped her arms around him and kissed him, knowing it wasn't going to go anywhere with her breakfast on the way but wishing it could. He kept kissing her, the minutes ticking away and her hunger for Callum building with each one, until she couldn't take it anymore.

Maybe just a quickie.

Kristina rolled him onto his back and kissed him harder, moaning as he grabbed her bottom and squeezed it, pressing her groin to his.

Someone knocked at the door.

"Breakfast," Callum said with a smile and pecked her cheek before lifting her off him.

She sat in the middle of the bed and frowned at his bottom as he walked around the foot of it and then into the bathroom to her left. He returned wearing a white terrycloth bathrobe and holding another one in his hand that he held out to her.

Kristina grabbed his wrist and tried to pull him back onto the bed but he shook his head, raised her hand to his mouth and kissed it.

"Food first... you need to keep your strength up." He grinned and walked out of the bedroom and disappeared around the corner of the living room.

She heard the door open, quickly donned her robe and roughly tied the belt around her waist, and then slid off the bed. She reached the open double doors to the living room just as a smartly dressed waiter pushed a large trolley into the room, and was followed by another.

They lined up the two carts next to each other, both laden with an array of elegant silver domed covers, and removed the covers one by one with a flourish to reveal scrumptious looking food.

There was everything she had ordered and, God, she wanted to eat it all, every last scrap.

The second waiter left and the first held a black leather folder out to Callum. He took it and signed the bottom of the print out it contained.

The younger man looked at them both, and then his eyes settled on her and he said something that made her want to fly across the room and bite him.

"Eating for two?"

Callum's dark eyebrows flew up and then he frowned at the waiter. The man's eyes slowly edged back to him as though he had sensed the wave of anger that swept outwards from the vampire and he hiccupped a laugh.

"I meant you and your lady, Sir... not anything like that." The human quickly closed the bill and backed out of the room, throwing a nervous smile her way.

Callum slammed the door in his face so hard that the walls shook.

"You look beautiful," he said as he turned to face her and Kristina blinked at his change in temper. No trace of anger laced his scent now and she couldn't miss the spark of hunger that lit his eyes as he raked them over her, as though he could see through the fluffy white robe to her bare body. "You have a breathtaking figure but the robe does swamp you a little and sort of hangs in a bad way. The disgusting little flea saw us and then the amount of food, and just made an arrogant presumption. He didn't know you had missed meals and we were fairly active last night..."

His dirty smile told her that she had lost him to memories of what they had got up to.

Callum was right though and she was just making up for missed meals and burned calories, not eating for a reason altogether more alarming.

She looked down at the robe sagging around her waist and tracked back over what he had said.

She looked pregnant?

Kristina immediately stripped out of the white bathrobe and threw it on the floor. Callum's eyebrows rose again and his grin widened.

"Do I look pregnant to you now?" she snapped and the desire in his eyes turned to confusion. He stared at her for long seconds and then his shoulders slumped and he smiled again, crossed the room to her, and picked up her robe.

He settled it around her shoulders. "No. We both know it isn't possible. Even if it were, which it isn't, it's not as though you would already be craving."

That was true. She hadn't thought of that before.

God, why was she getting so worked up about this?

Was it just because it was the reason she had run away from home, leaving everything she had ever known behind?

She pressed her hand to her stomach and breathed deeply through her nose, long soothing breaths.

No.

Her heart reasoned that she couldn't get the probability out of her mind because she feared that Callum would discard her the moment he could and she would end up as a single parent, just as her mother had been.

It had taken years for her mother to find the courage to confess that her father hadn't died before she was born as she had always told her.

He had used her mother when she was ripe for mating, when sexual intercourse with her would feel best, and then left her the second he had discovered she was bearing his child.

Her mother had suffered because of it.

Not only had it broken her heart and her will, but it had led to years of abuse from other pack members.

She had lost her place within the family. In the end, Kristina's father's cruelty had cost her mother her life. She had taken it forty years ago. The day after Kristina had celebrated reaching maturity and entering the pack hierarchy.

"Kristina?" Callum whispered and she shook herself and looked up at him. He frowned and brushed a thumb across her cheek. "Why are you crying? I didn't mean to make it sound as though you looked pregnant... you don't."

She smiled and scrubbed the heels of her hands across her face. "It isn't that. Just... bad memories... nothing that concerns you."

"It does concern me when you end up staring at me with a mixture of pain and anguish in your eyes as though I'm some sort of demon out to destroy you and then start crying."

Kristina slipped her arms back into the robe, pulled it closed, tied it tighter than before so she had a waist and didn't look pregnant, and casually walked past him to the trolleys of food. It really did look delicious but she had lost her appetite.

"Kristina?" Callum said, his tone harder this time, conveying the anger she could already sense in him.

He wanted an answer.

He wanted her to open up and confide in him, but she couldn't. The thought that she might share part of herself with him only for him to leave her as her father had left her mother, used and broken, petrified her too much.

"I said no personal stuff, remember?" She picked at the crispy rashers of bacon that filled one of the smaller plates and popped a piece into her mouth.

It was divine.

The salty flavour revived her hunger.

Callum caught her arm and whirled her on the spot to face him.

"I know you did... but I'm sorry... I want to know about you." The hard edge to his emerald eyes demanded that she tell him and she opened her mouth, teetered on the brink of letting it all flood out of her and finding comfort in his strong protective embrace, and then clamped her teeth shut and shook her head. "Why not? What are you so fucking afraid of? Are you afraid that this thing that's happening between us might get a little too real for you?"

She stared mutely at him.

He released her arm and paced away from her, his fingers trembling as they raked through his hair, his chest heaving with each breath that held his growing anger at bay. She could feel it in him, a volcanic rise within his straining body, threatening to slip beyond his control and erupt.

He turned on her and the darkness in his eyes receded, his voice softening, edged with desperation. "You think this doesn't scare me too? You think I'm not petrified of where this might lead? Do you honestly fucking believe I haven't spent the past two days wondering if you're just going to walk out on me? I don't know what you're thinking... and I feel so fucking weak around you... and I'm man enough to admit that scares the shit out of me. Christ, I kept waking up today fearing I would find you weren't there beside me in bed... fearing I'd wake alone. I held you so damned tight because I thought if I did, I would feel it if you tried to leave me and could wake and stop you."

He swallowed hard, his fists tight trembling balls at his sides, pinned there as though he was stopping himself from doing something he would regret.

What? Strike her?

Kristina frowned at her thoughts.

Why would that come to her first? How messed up was she?

Callum had been nothing but kind and gentle with her. The one time he had hurt her, it had been her own fault and he hadn't been in full control of himself. He hadn't meant it. The reason he was restraining himself was probably because he wanted to touch her and feared it would drive her away if he did.

"I can't do this," he said and her heart squeezed. He couldn't leave her. She didn't want him to go and she didn't want him to kick her out either. She opened her mouth to say so but he cut her off with an icy glare. "If this means nothing to you... if you can't let me get close to you... let me know you... then get the fuck out of my life now. I'd rather cut my losses here than let you get any deeper into my heart so you can break it when you finally run away from me."

"Callum." Kristina reached for him but he was already turning away, storming towards the bedroom. He swept his hand out in a way that warned her not to follow him and slammed the double doors.

Kristina sank to her knees in the middle of the living room.

She didn't like ultimatums, but for some reason this didn't feel like one.

He had laid himself bare before her, had confessed that this was already something to him and that he wanted it to be something special to her too, had made himself vulnerable so she felt that she could too.

She wrapped her arms around her chest and stared at the closed white doors, the barrier between her heart and his.

He wasn't the only one who was frightened by how this was making them feel.

She felt weak too, needed him so much after only a short period of time.

He had become vital to her so quickly. She had felt the need in his embrace as they had slept together, sensed his arm tighten like steel around her whenever she had moved, and had known it was because he had wanted her to stay there pressed against him until he woke. She hadn't realised why though.

She hadn't realised that she was so ridiculously afraid of any male getting too close to her that she had been on the verge of running away from one who made her feel so safe, who had protected her from her own kind, who brought her to life with his touch and made her smile for the first time in what seemed like forever.

She hadn't had much to smile about since her mother's suicide.

She couldn't remember the last time she had laughed or giggled. It came so naturally with Callum.

The shower switched on, humming low, and the sound of water slapping against tiles brought images of him naked and wet to mind.

Kristina sucked in a long deep breath and exhaled it slowly.

She picked herself up, mentally dusted herself off, and turned to the trolleys of no doubt very expensive food that Callum had kindly got for her.

Her gaze drifted across the living area to a small dining one that looked a little formal for her tastes. She set the food out on the coffee table instead, sat down on the striped dark blue and gold couch, and ate while she waited for Callum to emerge from the bedroom.

It was an hour later, or two servings of bacon, eggs, sausages, potatoes and tomatoes, pancakes, half the toast, two waffles with chocolate sauce and strawberries, and a glass of orange juice in food terms, that he finally made his reappearance.

She tensed when the doors behind her opened and swallowed her mouthful of food, waiting for him to say something.

He crossed the room, appearing to her left, and sat down in the armchair there. He swung his feet up onto the wooden coffee table and she couldn't resist a glance at him. A white towel rode low on his hips but other than that he was all delicious naked flesh.

"Still here I see." He scowled at her. "Well, that's some progress, I guess."

Kristina picked at her food, her appetite waning again. The apology she had practiced from the moment she had sat down to eat fled her mind and she found herself saying something surprising instead.

"I was thinking about my mum and all the shit she went through. That's why I was crying." Her olive branch confession probably did her more favours than a feeble apology ever would have. Callum sat up, balanced on the edge of his seat and turned to face her. He didn't press her to continue so she didn't panic, and it all flowed out of her. As naturally as everything else did when it came to him. "I never knew my father. He left mum when she got pregnant with me. I always thought she was a strong woman, that she handled it so well and hadn't let it hurt her. I realised I was wrong when I reached adulthood and entered the pack. She had just been strong for me... waiting until I was independent. Then she killed herself."

"Christ... I didn't know. If I had..."

"You would have what? Not been honest with me about your feelings? Let me continue to act like I was because I'm scared I'll end up like my mother? I had to grow up sometime, Callum, and you couldn't have known... so don't blame yourself. You said what had to be said... and I do actually appreciate it... because now I know I'm not the only one who is scared crapless about this."

She risked another glance at him and the steel in his green eyes was gone, replaced by a feather soft and warm look that filled her with a need to go to him, settle herself on his lap and beg him to just hold her for a while and tell her that her craziness hadn't ruined everything.

"Is that why you ran away from your pack?"

She shook her head. She might as well be honest about that too.

"I ran away because our alpha got it into his head that he wanted me to bear his offspring and I wanted nothing to do with it. Pack laws state he's within his rights to force me to go through with it. He tried to do just that... even had his second in command help him pin me down so he could mark me and chain me to him... so I attacked him and fled. I've been running ever since."

Callum's growl was so low it was almost inaudible.

She felt it as a rumble through her, a possessive purr that sent sparks racing over her nerve endings. He rose from his seat, sat down next to her, and tugged her into his arms, clutching her head to his chest.

His heart pounded quickly against her ear.

"I won't let them near you, Kristina... and I won't hurt you like that bastard did to your mother. You don't have to run anymore. Just... let me protect you. I can take you somewhere you will be safe. I can protect you."

Kristina relaxed against him and closed her eyes, feeling the truth in his words in her heart.

Callum was different and she believed him when he said that he would keep her safe, and that he could keep her safe. He was strong enough. Not even her alpha would be able to stand up to him.

"So... you certainly weren't wrong when you ordered enough food to feed a starving village."

She frowned, drew back, and turned her scowl on him. He merely smiled, pushed a hank of her wavy hair behind her ear, and looked at the remaining food.

"What does it taste like?" he said with curiosity lighting his eyes as much as his smile.

"You mean you really can't eat?"

He shook his head. "Like I said, not a sausage."

It was her turn to smile and tease. "So how the hell am I supposed to tell you what food tastes like? You live on a blood only diet. Even if I said things like salty, or spicy, or the sausage is scrummy because it has herbs to complement the pork... you wouldn't have a clue what I'm talking about."

He looked disappointed. "Can't you at least try? I can't ingest food but I know what some alcohol tastes like. Only sips though, or I end up craving more blood."

Kristina stared at all the delicious food, wishing she was skilled enough with words to explain every subtle nuance of its taste and how it made her feel so Callum could experience it too. He'd had sips of alcohol. Did that mean he could taste things in liquid form? Solids would prove a problem for him so anything other than the orange juice was probably off the menu.

Unless.

She picked up a piece of bacon, stuffed it into her mouth, chewed on it a long time and then swallowed it and used her tongue to check that every morsel was gone.

Callum stared at the plate.

Kristina moved onto her knees beside him, caught his cheek, brought his mouth around to hers and kissed him.

It was worth a shot.

He delved his tongue into her mouth and moaned softly when she withdrew before he could get her motor revving again.

"Well?" she said and he looked blankly at her. "How did I taste?"

His dark eyebrows met in a frown. "Salty. See I can tell the difference. Oh." He cracked a grin. "Wicked wicked girl. Eat something else."

Was he trying to get her fat?

She had already eaten enough food for a starving village as he had so carefully and kindly put it. She balanced on the brink of telling him to just lick the food himself or risk chewing it and then spitting it out, but the beautiful look of childish excitement on his face had her relenting.

He picked up a plate of strawberries.

"Eat these. I want to know if they taste like that gloss I kissed off you last night. I know the smell of them, what they're called, but I don't know their real taste." He took a plump round strawberry off the plate and shoved it at her. At least it was lower in calories than all the other food. Callum fixed that. He took it from her before she could bite into it, swirled it around in the chocolate sauce, and grinned as he returned it to her mouth. "Eat it now. I want to know what chocolate tastes like too."

She bit into it, chewed and then swallowed.

The moment it was gone from her mouth, Callum was kissing her, experiencing the delicious combination of chocolate and strawberry on her tongue.

He didn't stop there.

He reached for a different food and Kristina found herself having to try a little piece of everything all over again so he could kiss her afterwards and comment on how she had tasted.

She had created a monster.

By the time they had tried everything, she was so full that she wanted a cat nap to sleep it off.

"We could order dinner," Callum said and she covered his mouth with her hand and shook her head.

"I'm going to shower and never eat again. If I come out and find you've ordered more food, I will scream. Understand?"

He nodded.

She released his mouth.

He grinned at her.

"What if I helped you burn off the calories?"

CHAPTER 7

Callum was insatiable.

Not just in the bedroom, but when it came to food too. Each day he ordered different things from the hotel menu and insisted on feeding them to her. She had tried to convince him to just lick the food himself but he hadn't gone for it. Breakfast. Lunch. Dinner. Every meal was spent with him kissing her between bites.

And at the end of it, when all those kisses had wound her so tight inside that she had come close to bursting and jumping on him more than once, they made out like teenagers on the couch.

Almost a week had passed and she hadn't dressed in all that time or left the suite.

They had been together the whole time, learning about each other's bodies and pasts, about things they had in common and things they felt completely the opposite about.

Callum had only left her side once since her arrival at his hotel and she had missed him like crazy even though he had only been gone for little more than an hour in order to feed.

He had returned with a bag full of naughty things and a vodka bottle full of blood for her, offering it with a charming smile and a flourish as though it was a bottle of the finest Dom Perignon. Her stomach had growled so loud at the sight and smell of it that she had blushed a shade of red darker than the blood.

She hadn't thought to ask who it had come from or how the heck he had got it into the bottle. She had eagerly watched him pour it into two glasses and had swallowed hers in one gulp, causing Callum to laugh at her and refill it.

The sex they'd had after that had been as wild and hungry as their first time together.

The sound of water splashing into the tub brought her back to her present location. Candles cast a warm flickering glow around the normally austere white bathroom, filling it with the soothing scent of vanilla.

Callum sat behind her in the immense corner tub with her between his long legs, his hands lazily running up and down her arms, occasionally dipping into the water and bringing the soapy suds up over her chest.

He cupped her breasts, thumbing her nipples, and she relaxed against him.

It wasn't the first time they had bathed together, but it was the first time they had lasted more than ten minutes without making out.

"This is nice," she murmured and closed her eyes, running her hands over his muscular thighs where they pressed against hers and skimming her fingers over his knees.

He laughed and wriggled.

It had taken her only three days to discover his knees were ticklish.

She had mercilessly abused the knowledge until he had realised that it only took the barest brush of his finger anywhere close to her armpit for her to burst into hysterical giggles and collapse in a heap.

"It is nice," he echoed and softly kissed her shoulder.

He felt relaxed on her senses and she was glad she wasn't the only one enjoying just spending time together in this way. The sex was fantastic, she couldn't get enough of him, but it was moments like this that were firmly becoming her favourite times with Callum.

She sighed and wrapped her hands under his thighs.

Did that mean what she feared it did?

Was she falling in love with him?

She barely knew him. Her heart said that didn't matter. They had passed the most incredible week together and had shared so much in that time, opening to each other by degrees.

"Have you ever had a werewolf lover?" She stroked the underside of his thighs beneath the water, feeling the fine hairs on them and his strong sinewy muscles.

"Not before you. What about you?" He swept his lips over her shoulder again and moved his hands down to her stomach. She shivered when his fingertips brushed close to her groin and sighed as he moved away again.

Tease.

Kristina laughed. "One or two."

"Better than me?" He sounded so serious that she laughed again and he reprimanded her with a light tap against her stomach, sending waves rippling outwards from his arm.

They broke against her knees above the waterline and bounced back against her.

"No." She smiled. "You're quite the catch. What about human lovers?"

"None." He kissed the curve of her throat, his fingers tickling as he brushed aside the wet strands of her hair that stuck to her skin.

"Vampires?"

"Of course."

She hesitated for a beat. "Do you have one at the moment?"

"No!" The hardness in that word as he snapped it close to her ear caused her to tense. Anger rippled across her senses, warning that she had offended him and was coming close to ruining this pleasant quiet moment between them. "Of course not. I'm not that sort of man, Kristina. I haven't had a lover of any sort in a long time... definitely nothing serious since I started Vampirerotique with the others."

"Vampirerotique?" Kristina leaned to one side and tried to look at him over her shoulder. "What's that?"

"A theatre in London. We put on performances for vampire clientele... erotic shows."

Her eyebrows flew up. "So that's where you learned your tricks."

She had wondered how he had learned to do some of the things that they had experienced together. He knew positions she had never realised were possible.

"No." He shook his head. "I don't even watch the shows. I just scout for performers."

"Is that what brought you to Paris?"

He nodded. "It was. I haven't checked in since first setting eyes on you."

"Oh, really?" Kristina turned in the tub, sending water sloshing back and forth, and came to kneel between his legs. She lifted her hand from the water and stroked his chest. Bubbly rivulets ran down from her fingertips, cascading over the honed peaks and valleys of his torso. He looked delicious all wet and soapy, his long black hair slicked back and his arms resting on the sides of the white tub, surrounded by flickering candlelight. Very decadent. The perfect appearance for an owner of a naughty club. "All this time you've had a mind for only business since starting some dirty theatre with your pals—"

"I assure you, it's quite tasteful."

"I bet. How long ago did you first open?"

"Around a century." His eyelids drooped as she swirled her index fingers around his nipples and then flicked open again.

"That's almost as old as I am." She paused and stared at him.

He had been running some naughty club for a century. That was a lot of time to spend around erotic acts and not watch them.

If he sourced the performers, surely he would want to see that they turned out good and satisfied the crowd?

"So, in one hundred years, you've just had your mind on business... fixated on it... no time for little Cal to come out and play..." She ran her hand over his soft cock beneath the water and it twitched against her palm, rising under her caress. "And now you've gone AWOL?"

"Because of you," he hissed from between his teeth and the cords of his neck tautened. "How old are you?"

"That's not the important thing here. You really ditched work because of me?" She kept up her stroking, loving the pained look on Callum's face as he tried to focus on speaking to her rather than what her hand was doing.

His cock broke the surface of the water, rigid and eager, wet and glistening in the candlelight.

Kristina found her concentration slipping, the temptation to move to kneel astride his hips and sink down onto his beautiful erection shattering it.

"I really did. I told you I couldn't think straight and you drove me crazy." He smiled tightly and then groaned and rubbed his cock against her palm. "I meant it."

"Well, I'm flattered." She shifted her hand to his chest, leaned in and kissed him long and slow. Callum pressed his hand to her shoulder and pushed her backwards.

"So how old are you?" He wasn't letting that one go.

"One hundred and twelve." Kristina sat back again and he raked his emerald eyes over her. They lingered on her breasts and then rose back to her face.

"Really. So young?"

She shrugged. "I look older. I hear that a lot. It's the boobs."

"You do have fantastic tits." He cupped both of them in his cool hands and squeezed, his eyes darkening.

Kristina caught him under the chin and tipped his head up again to get his attention.

"How old are you?" she said.

"Mid five hundreds." He said it as though it was nothing.

"You old fart," she teased with a grin and he moved so fast she barely saw it.

He grabbed her wrist, pulled her body against his, so their torsos pressed together, his rigid cock against her stomach, and kissed her. Water sloshed over the edge of the tub and broke against her bottom, waves rocking back and forth until they finally dwindled.

When he released her, she slumped against him, a little dizzy and tired from lack of air, but humming with satisfaction and heat.

"I didn't hear you complaining earlier when you were bucking like a wild animal beneath me and screaming my name at the top of your lungs." He grinned at her.

Kristina blushed.

He had knelt in the middle of the large bed, holding her bottom high off it with her legs in the air, his hips pumping hard and fast, driving his cock into her while she lay helpless at a diagonal, breasts bouncing with each thrust.

It had felt so damned good.

The man could match her strength and passion, even took her beyond her limit sometimes, and each time it felt phenomenal.

She lifted one of his hands off her breasts and looked at his fingers. "You're going wrinkly."

How long had they been in the bath?

She held his gaze and slowly curled three of his fingers over, leaving his index finger extended, and sucked it into her mouth.

Callum growled and frowned, his gaze darting to her mouth. She swirled her tongue around the tip of his finger, teasing him, and then moved it in and out, sucking it harder.

Callum pulled his hand free, stood so fast that water splashed out of the tub again and across the tiles, and snatched hold of her wrist. He dragged her to her feet, kissed her hard, and then lifted her effortlessly out of the tub.

She skidded on the soaked tiles and grabbed one of the towels, laying it down to absorb the wet and give them some grip. She moved forwards and grabbed another towel to place on the floor there.

He stepped up behind her, slid his hands over her hips, and nestled his hard cock against her bottom. She froze and closed her eyes when he bent his knees and dropped lower, rubbing his length against her pussy.

It seemed little Cal was making up for all the years his master had neglected him.

Kristina straightened and her eyes widened when she found herself faced with her reflection in the full length mirror at the end of the bathroom.

Patchy fog covered some parts of her body but she didn't notice them.

She was too captivated by the vision of her stood naked and wet with Callum behind her. He kissed her shoulder, his eyes on hers in the mirror, and caressed her sides. His fingers brushed the underside of her breasts and she leaned her back against his chest, her eyelids falling to half mast.

His thumbs came up, flicking the already hard buds of her nipples, and she groaned.

He held her gaze in the mirror, wicked looking as he stood behind her, his body obscured by hers. He dipped down and ground against her backside, his eyes darkening with each rub of his cock.

Seeing the pleasure in his eyes only made the thought of making love to him like this, watching him thrusting into her, seeing his cock appear and disappear, all the more appealing.

Kristina wriggled her bottom against him and he gasped, growled and then grabbed her hips and pulled her hard against his cock. He wedged it tight into the crack of her backside and gave a few wild thrusts. Her breasts bounced with each one.

He slid his right hand down from her hip and it was her turn to gasp as he slipped it into her soft folds, seeking her heat. He pressed two fingers against her clit and then eased lower.

Kristina tiptoed, leaning on him for support, and groaned as he dipped his two fingers into her sheath, drawing her arousal out of her, and brought it up to her clit. He lazily circled it, flicking occasionally, and teased her breasts with his other hand. His mouth worked on her throat, each kiss and nip heightening the pleasure she felt from his touch.

He ground against her again, harder this time, drawing his hips back and thrusting forwards. The blunt head of his cock nudged her anus and she groaned and shivered.

Callum groaned too and shifted backwards.

She frowned at the loss of contact and then her disappointment melted away when he turned her to one side and pushed her forwards.

Kristina bent over and pressed her hands against the damp wall tiles to support herself. She looked across at their reflections, moaning as Callum moved behind her, his impressive cock jutting towards her, hard and ready.

She couldn't take her eyes off him as he took his right hand and slid it over her pussy, dragging it down from her slick opening to her clit and pausing there.

He stroked the nub, pushing her a little closer to the edge with each light caress, until she was moaning with each barely-there sweep of his fingers, and then eased his hand upwards again.

She raised her hips in supplication, silently begging him to enter her.

She wanted to see that long cock sliding slowly into her body and feel it stretching her at the same time. She wanted to watch him withdraw it and fuck her, see his bottom tensing and quivering with each wild pump of his hips.

He eased his fingers back inside her, all the way this time, and pumped her slowly with them. She moaned and tensed her fingers against the tiles.

Callum looked across at the mirror and groaned too, his eyes on his hand and then on her as she watched him. He pulled his fingers out of her and she thought he would finally plunge his cock into her, but he dragged them upwards instead.

She shivered and groaned as he smeared her own arousal over her anus and then dipped back inside her to gather more. He slathered it over her puckered hole and then stuck his thumb into her hot sheath. Anticipation stole her breath. She hadn't done this sort of thing with a man before and she hoped that Callum would be gentle with her. He met her gaze and clearly saw her nerves because he smiled warmly at her.

He pulled his thumb free of her, took hold of his cock with his left hand, and brought the crown of it to her warm core.

Kristina groaned in perfect timing with Callum as he entered her, drawing out the experience. She stared at his cock, watching it sliding in and filling her. It was the most erotic thing she had ever seen.

She kept her gaze glued to the point where their bodies joined as Callum withdrew almost all of his cock and then slowly entered her again.

She moaned.

That was his beautiful cock filling her, sending ripples of pleasure through her with each long stroke.

She couldn't quite get over the sight.

He built the pace between them and she still stared, feeling him plunge into her core as well as see it, alternating between watching the pleasure crossing his face and his cock. He met her gaze as she glanced up at his face in the mirror and groaned, pumping her harder.

The thought that he was watching them too, that they were both watching how their bodies fit together, sent her arousal soaring.

He ran his right hand over her bottom and she was so absorbed in watching his cock pumping into her, his buttocks tensing with each hard thrust, that she didn't notice what he was doing.

At first, she thought it was just the shift in position he made that caused the startling tingles that shot through her, but then she felt something push deeper.

Kristina gasped and her gaze shot to her bottom.

Callum pressed his thumb to her anus and edged it inside. She couldn't tell how much. The feel of it in combination with the feel of his cock plunging into her was too much pleasure for her to handle. She moaned, writhed, tried to keep her eyes open and fixed on what he was doing, knowing her orgasm would be the most incredible experience if she did. Callum withdrew his length and thrust into her again, his thick shaft disappearing into her body, and she screamed out her climax.

Everything went hazy for a few seconds, Callum's thrusts not slowing, his left hand holding her fast as he pumped into her, and then came back.

Callum eased his thumb out and then in a little deeper, the pace of his movements different to his wild thrusts. She moaned and her knees trembled, threatening to give out.

"Take me to the bed," she whispered.

He pulled out of her, scooped her into his arms, and carried her to the bed. She sighed as he laid her down on it and rolled onto her front, raising her bottom so he could continue with what he had been doing. She didn't want him to stop. Not when it felt so good and he hadn't found release yet.

Callum rubbed her bottom.

"Kristina," he whispered and she looked over her shoulder at him. The dark hunger in his eyes told her what he wanted and she nodded, wanting to experience it too.

He positioned her on her front and then went to the bedside table. He grabbed the bottle of lubricant and the bullet vibrator he had bought during his outing and came back to her. She relaxed into the bed, sated from her orgasm, ready to melt.

The lubricant was cold on her bottom but soon warmed as Callum rubbed her, teasing her with shallow presses of his fingers inside her. He pushed his fingers back into her hot core, reigniting her desire, sending her heart fluttering. She writhed and moaned, desire taking control of her again, making her seek another release.

Kristina looked over her shoulder when he withdrew his fingers and she groaned as he slathered every inch of his cock with the lubricant. He moved over her, raised her bottom off the bed, and opened her with one hand while positioning himself with his other. She bit her lip at the first nudge of the blunt head of his cock against her anus. His gaze met hers and he pressed a little deeper. She sank her teeth into her lower lip. It stung as he nudged further in and he stilled. It felt as though he was tearing her apart.

He lowered his other hand to her clit and teased it.

"Relax," he whispered and swirled his fingers around her, distracting her from the tight pain.

"Does it always hurt?"

He smiled. "I don't know. I've never done it before."

Kristina's eyebrows rose. A first for both of them.

He squeezed more lubricant onto his cock and her, and eased a little deeper inside. The pain started to fade but it still stung. The feel of his fingers pinching and teasing her clit kept her mind off it though.

Callum grunted and she moaned when he withdrew a few inches and then plunged deeper.

God.

His fingers danced over her, keeping her balanced on the edge, and he pressed harder into her. She moaned hoarsely at the same time as him, feeling the rest of his cock slide into her anus. The pain subsided as he slowly moved out of her and then back in, his fingers shifting to her core. He plunged the small vibrator into her, the dual penetration sending a shiver through her, and she groaned into the pillow.

Each slow stroke of his cock into her backside tore an animalistic grunt from Callum and sent her quivering. His pace built gently, a little quicker and harder with each stroke, his tempo still discordant with his thrusts of the vibrator into her warm sheath. She moaned and clutched the bedclothes, clinging to them, head reeling with pleasure and how surprisingly good it felt to have his cock penetrating her anus, stretching her body.

Callum released the vibrator, leaving it buzzing inside her sheath, and his fingers moved to her clit again and he rubbed it. It was too much for her.

Kristina came undone, violent trembles racking her and his name falling hoarsely from her lips. He thrust deeper into her, hips pumping faster as her body relaxed beneath him, and then cried close to her ear as he climaxed, flooding her with his cool seed. His cock pulsed as he settled against her back, still buried deep in her body and the vibrator still buzzing, sending hot shivers of desire pulsing outwards from her core.

She turned her face towards him and looked at him out of the corner of her eye. He licked a spot on the back of her shoulder and she shivered, ached for him to go through with what he wanted to do. He glanced at her, paused, and then sank his fangs into her shoulder.

Kristina cried out, body bucking against his, and climaxed again. Burning waves crashed through her and Callum groaned behind her, his teeth buried as deep in her flesh as his cock was. She moaned and writhed, drugged by the feel of him taking her blood into him, by how it felt to be so possessed by him. She wanted to possess him too.

She groped around, painfully twisting her arm to reach his. She grabbed his wrist, pulled it to her, and sank her fangs into his forearm, biting hard into his soft flesh.

His blood burst onto her tongue, strong and intoxicating, and he grunted against her back and thrust into her.

The feel of his cock pulsing again, his seed flowing into her, and his slowing pulls on her blood, as well as the encroaching fuzzy darkness at the edge of her vision, warned what was coming.

She managed only a single mouthful of blood before the darkness claimed her.

When Kristina came around, Callum was lying next to her on the bed, naked and spent, his soft cock resting against her hip. He was awake.

“We really should stop biting during sex,” he said with a lazy sated smile. “How are you feeling?”

“Incredible.” She stretched, noting that she was under the covers now and that the vibrator stood beside her on the table, and that she was clean again. Callum must have taken care of her. She sank into the soft bed, feeling as though she had slept for days. “How long was I out?”

“It’s gone nine. Only an hour.” He ran a hand over her shoulder and she shivered when his fingers brushed the bite mark there. “You taste divine.”

“Mmm, you too. Better than anything I’ve had the pleasure of drinking before.” She rolled onto her side, leaned over and lightly swept her lips over his.

He moaned and pushed her backwards. “You’re giving him the wrong impression.”

She glanced down at his cock. It was already semi-hard. She stroked it, teasing him and enjoying the way he growled and frowned at her. He took her hand away from his penis and slapped it.

“Why not?” Kristina pouted.

He smiled, charming and handsome, his green eyes bright with it. “Because I want to take you out to dinner.”

“Really?” Kristina stared at him. Like a real date? “What are you going to do during this date? Just sit there and watch me?”

“And kiss you,” he said with a wider smile. “Bathe and dress.”

Kristina nodded, went to the bathroom and took a quick shower. It was only when she was stepping out of it that she remembered she only had one set of clothes with her. She wrapped the towel around herself and walked back into the bedroom.

Callum was still lounging on the bed in all his naked glory. It was hard to muster the desire to go out when he looked so temptingly tasty.

"I have nothing to wear to a restaurant," she said and he frowned across the room at her.

"I can order you something."

From the hotel? Kristina didn't like the sound of that. He ordered everything for her and she was beginning to feel like a kept woman, not the independent one she had decided to be. She shook her head and he sat up.

"How about I get dressed, go back to my hotel, and pick up my things. I have the perfect dress for that ridiculously expensive restaurant I expect you have in mind."

He grinned as though amused that she could see straight through him too and then a strange fire lit his eyes and he held his hand out to her. She went to him, slipped her hand into his, and let him lead her onto the bed. He kissed her, his hands firm against her sides, and was still smiling when he drew back.

"All your things?" he said, his smile holding.

Kristina realised what he meant and that it made him happy. He wanted her to come and stay with him, and wanted her to go with him when he had to leave. She wanted that too. She nodded. "Every last thing."

He kissed her again, a brief hard press of his lips, and then patted her backside. "Hurry."

She slipped off the bed, dressed quickly, and tied her mac around her waist. "Wait for me."

Callum walked with her to the door and kissed her again, slower this time, a soft one that warmed her right down to the marrow of her bones.

"I'm not going anywhere," he whispered against her lips and stroked her cheek before kissing her again.

Kristina smiled and backed off, giggling as she did so. If she didn't go now, she would never make it back before the restaurants closed.

She almost made it out of the door before she came back and kissed him again, reluctant to leave his side. He laughed and she clenched her fists.

"I'm really going this time." She pecked his cheek and headed out, resisting the temptation to look back as she walked down the corridor and see if he was watching her.

She made it down to the lobby and out onto the pavement. The doorman there hailed a taxi for her and she stepped into it.

A man got in the other door.

"This cab's taken," she said and then frowned when her senses blared in warning.

She looked across at the dark haired man, unable to make his face out in the shadows. Vampire. He smiled at her, flashing fangs, and slapped a hand down on her thigh so hard it stung.

"I've been waiting for you to leave that place all week," he said in a strange foreign accented voice and her vision wavered, sound swimming in her ears. She looked down at the hand on her thigh and blinked.

A silver tube with feathers protruded from her leg.

A dart.

"What the?" she said and collapsed against the man. The last thing she made out before she slipped into unconsciousness was a single word.

"Aéroport."

CHAPTER 8

It was Antoine's order to return to Vampirerotique in time for the special performance that had finally forced Callum to leave Paris. He had waited for Kristina to return from gathering her things.

Hours had passed before he realised that she wasn't coming back and had gone out in search of her.

He didn't know where her hotel was so he had gone to the club where they had first made love. The three male werewolves had been there, and none of them had been pleased to see him.

At first, he had suspected that they had waylaid her, but they had soon proven that theory false. A brief fight with them had convinced them that he meant business and it would be best to answer his questions if they wanted to live to see another night. When they had, their scents and heartbeats had remained calm. They hadn't been the ones to take her. He had faltered then, his faith shaken and heart aching, briefly convinced that she had finally run away from him.

He had cursed himself then. He should have gone with her, should have escorted her to her hotel, waited for her to change and get her things, and then dropped them back at his hotel before heading out for dinner. It had been foolish of him to let her go alone.

The largest male werewolf had mentioned her pack and Callum had remembered that she was on the run from her family.

Could they have found her?

It had only taken another brief tussle to convince the werewolf to supply the names of the hotels in Paris that his species frequented, driven by their pack instinct to remain together even when they were different families.

Callum had checked them all and had success at one of them. She had been staying there. In fact, her clothes had still been there and the manager had been fairly irritated that she had apparently disappeared before paying.

He had paid for her room and taken her belongings with him. On each of the next four nights, he had taken a deep breath of her scent that lingered on her clothes and gone out in search of her.

If she had run, she would have taken her belongings. Someone had snatched her.

It had to be her pack.

The werewolves in Paris had grown tired and snappish, annoyed by the questions he fired whenever he came across one. He had built quite the reputation for himself as an irritating take-no-shit vampire by the time Antoine had called him and commanded him to return to London. Antoine had refused to listen to reason. His order was final.

Callum's flight had landed at the City Airport just forty minutes ago. The limousine had already pulled up outside the warmly lit columned façade of the old theatre building but he had yet to find the strength to leave it. It felt as though he would leave all hope of finding her behind when he did.

No.

There was always hope.

If her pack had taken her, then he would go to every werewolf family in Britain in search of her. He would find her and take her back. She was his now.

She was his everything.

These past few nights without her had been a test of his strength. He had relentlessly searched for her, driven by his need to find her and protect her, to have her back in his arms. Each night that had passed had worn him down a little more, stealing a fraction of his hope and his strength. He felt close to collapse now, lost and adrift, unable to function while Kristina was out there somewhere, probably scared and waiting for him to come for her. He had to find her.

As soon as he had spoken to Antoine, he would take the limousine and head out again. He would start tonight, not losing a second in his search for her. He wouldn't relent until he had found her and she was safe in his arms again.

His Kristina.

"Wait for me here," he said and stepped out of the black car. The pavement outside the theatre was quiet. He left his belongings in the car and went through the glass doors and into the gold and red foyer. It was empty too.

The hour was growing late. The performance would already be underway.

Callum took the side door that led backstage and walked down the darkly painted corridor that ran the length of the theatre. He wasn't in the mood to make an appearance in the stalls of the theatre and Antoine always lingered near the doors that opened onto the gangway between the front row of seats and the stage.

Callum reached the large black-walled double-height area where steps led upstairs and another corridor led backstage. He pushed open the double doors and spotted Antoine nearby, his pale blue eyes fixed on the stage.

The aristocrat vampire glanced at him, frowned and then walked over to him. Callum stepped into the theatre and eased the doors closed behind him. Antoine raked long fingers through the lengths of his dark hair and his frown hardened. Callum ignored the erotic sounds coming from the stage and looked at the audience. It wasn't a full house. That in itself was unusual.

What made Callum pause was the sight of thick steel bars edging the stage, turning it into a huge cage.

What sort of performance was Antoine putting on tonight in front of this select crowd?

It was all aristocrats in the seats. Normally the stalls were full of the elite and the aristocrats remained aloft in their boxes.

"What's going on?" Callum looked back at Antoine.

"I could ask you the same thing," the aristocrat snapped and his look darkened. "Where the Devil have you been? You have been gone twice as long as you should have and haven't contacted me in more than a week. Do I not have enough to worry about without you adding to it?"

Callum mumbled his apology.

Antoine huffed and looked back at the stage. "It is a special performance. Lord and Lady Hallebrand requested it for their youngest son's birthday. I do not know much else about it besides that. They requested we provide the theatre and the performers. That was all. It turns out they decided to provide some performers of their own too... and when you failed to report in and provide further werewolves for auditions, they set about sourcing some themselves so the performance could go ahead."

Callum frowned at the stage and the two couples fornicating on the other side. It didn't look much different to the normal show they put on each week.

There were long chains and shackles bolted to the floor though, and one of the men was using them on his woman, bending her forwards with her ankles and wrists securely fastened so she couldn't move as he fucked her from behind. The position sent flashes of his moment with Kristina in the bathroom across his eyes and he drew in a deep breath.

It was then he caught the scent of werewolf.

Were the couples on stage werewolves? He didn't recognise any of them from his scouting mission but then he rarely paid close enough attention to potential performers for him to remember them once they reached his stage, and Antoine had mentioned that the couple had also sourced performers.

He looked back at Antoine.

The aristocrat vampire was glaring at the stage, his displeasure rolling off him in tangible waves. Something had annoyed him, and Callum had the feeling it wasn't his disappearing act.

Was it the show that had him more agitated than usual or had something happened with Snow again?

Whenever Snow was going through a bad patch, Antoine turned into a bear with a one-track mind bent on bloody murder. Callum normally requested he be allowed out to scout for new performers whenever Antoine got into one of those moods and left Javier to deal with him.

The performance ended and when the curtain rose again there was a large box-shaped object in the middle of the stage, draped in a black velvet cloth. It shifted as though someone was underneath it. The audience murmured, their excitement lacing the air.

The veil covering the box rose, revealing a steel cage and three naked women huddled in the centre. One blonde, one brunette.

And Kristina.

Callum snarled.

Kristina turned her hazel eyes in his direction and ran at the bars, growling and trying to reach him. "You bastard!"

His heart stopped dead. Ice filled his veins. She thought he had betrayed her. Her pain ran in his blood, conveying her disappointment and anger.

Three large male vampires entered the stage, wearing only tight black jeans, each one carrying a black bull-whip.

The audience jeered.

The gate of the cage lifted and then one man stepped forwards, thrust his hand into the cage and grabbed the blonde werewolf by her throat. He dragged her kicking and screaming out into the middle of the stage and threw her to one side. His whip cracked across her back a moment later, sending her arching forwards and screaming as a bright red streak appeared and the scent of her blood filled the air. The audience gasped and leaned forwards as one, eager for more.

Callum growled and ran at the stage, leaping up to balance on the edge. He gripped the thick steel bars and tried to pull them apart, snarling and verging on losing control. The steel bars started to give and his heart lurched when a second vampire dragged the brunette werewolf out of the cage by her hair, pulling her across the stage on her backside.

The third male approached the cage.

Kristina backed into the far corner, growling and snarling at the vampire.

"Kristina!" Callum called out and she turned fearful teary eyes on him. He reached out to her through the bars, desperate to get through to her so he could protect her from the man.

"What the hell are you doing?" Antoine grabbed his ankle and dragged him down. He toppled and hit the red carpet with a sharp thud.

He was on his feet again and reaching for the steel bars before a beat had passed. Antoine grabbed his upper arm, fingers pressing painfully through the layers of his black shirt and jacket. Callum snarled and shoved him away. Antoine's pale blue eyes turned glacial and then began to turn red.

"She's my lover!" Callum snapped and gave up on trying to make it through the steel bars. He wasn't strong enough. He crashed through the double doors instead and banked left, sprinting for the door that led onto the stage.

He tore it open and ran out into the fray. All three vampire males sported wounds now and a good deal of blood coated the black stage floor, turning it slippery. He ran forwards, past the now transformed female werewolves.

One of the male vampires lashed out at him with the whip and Callum caught it by the tip before it could strike him, twisted it around his arm, and pulled it out of the man's grip.

He wrapped his fingers around the thick handle, twirled it in the air above his head, and sent it at the man who had attacked him. It cracked across his chest, leaving a bloody streak. The vampire snarled at him and Callum roared back.

The audience started to jeer louder, as though this was all part of the act. Two voices rang out above the noise though, protesting loudly about what he was doing.

Callum didn't listen.

He cracked the whip again, keeping the three men at bay. The wolves gathered behind him, growling and snarling, their hackles raised. Callum glanced at all three of them. He didn't know which one was Kristina. The smell of their spilled blood combined and he couldn't pick hers out.

"Kristina." He cracked the whip again when one of the vampires tried to rush him. He didn't recognise any of them. Antoine had said that the lord and lady responsible for this horror show had brought some of their own performers. These men had to be theirs. Everyone at Vampirerotique knew him and knew not to mess with him. "Stay back. I'll protect you."

The wolves growled behind him and it didn't sound like a favourable response.

Two launched past him, one on either side, and locked their jaws on to two of the vampires. One man went down with a werewolf on his arm. The other was less fortunate. The female had a good aim and bit into his throat, sending blood gushing down his broad bare chest. He hit the floor and struggled in vain.

The other vampire shook off the werewolf who had attacked him and Callum attacked the third. He dropped the whip and launched himself at the man, slashing his claws down his chest and spilling blood. The man punched him several times across the jaw, sending his head spinning. Callum didn't relent. He clawed at the man between punching and dodging, weakening him by spilling his blood.

Another werewolf attacked the male that had fallen, tearing at him.

The vampire who had been bitten on the arm barrelled into Callum and sent him crashing into the hard black wall at the back of the stage. Callum kicked out as the man reached him, catching him hard in the balls, and he hit the deck.

"Enough!" Antoine's voice cut through the cacophony of shouts, jeers, snarls and growls. The sound of steel creaking under pressure had Callum, the two remaining male vampires, and the three wolves stopping and turning towards the source of the sound.

Antoine pulled the thick steel bars apart with his bare hands as though they were made of rubber. The formidable display of strength and the rage rolling off the powerful aristocrat vampire had everyone on stage staring, the fight forgotten. The three female werewolves slunk back towards the corner, gathering into a group so tight that the brown, black and tan of their fur blended together.

Antoine stepped through the bars and frowned at his dirtied hands and then at the two male vampires.

"I have allowed this to go on long enough," he said, the calm edge to his tone unsettling Callum.

He sidestepped away from the two vampires, experience making him move. He had seen Antoine in a foul mood and normally when he sounded as calm as he did now, it ended in bloodshed and then death for some unfortunate soul.

A squat fair haired man came to the edge of the stage. "Explain what is happening here!"

Antoine turned icy eyes on him. "The performance is off. I never would have agreed to this if I had realised this sick show was your intention. You requested performers, not victims. I consider that a contravention of our agreement. I suggest you and your companions leave before I decide to make everyone pay for bringing such a depraved and disgusting act into my theatre."

The man didn't move.

Antoine roared.

A few seconds later, Snow burst through the double doors, broken chains rattling against the thick metal and leather cuffs around his wrists, his overlong white hair bright in the darkness of the theatre.

Javier rushed in behind him, wearing only his black trousers, closely followed by Lilah. Her chestnut hair was wet and her black bathrobe swamped her slender figure.

Snow looked around, eyes wild and searching, his broad bare chest heaving as he dragged in deep breaths, and spotted the source of his brother's irritation. He snarled, his eyes flashing bright crimson.

Lord Hallebrand moved then, backing away from the immense, snarling vampire heading towards him. Snow was older than most aristocrats, his strength twice that of his younger brother Antoine, and his power unsurpassable. The audience made a break for it, fleeing towards the exits, leaving Lord and Lady Hallebrand and their son to fend for themselves.

Javier caught Snow's arm and pulled him back, tugging on the broken restraints. It looked as though he was trying to restrain a three hundred pound attack dog as he grappled with a snarling vicious Snow, taking a few blows in the process.

Lilah leapt in front of Snow.

"Lilah, no!" Javier shouted with obvious distress at the thought of Snow hurting her.

The hulking mass of vampire stopped dead, his glowing red eyes on her, his snarls lowering to rumbling growls.

Javier clung to Snow's arms, holding them both behind his back, his dark eyes pinned to the back of Snow's head, watching him. Callum didn't doubt that he would seek to wound Snow if the vampire dared to even attempt to harm his mate. The Spaniard was fiercely protective of her, and Callum could understand why now that he had a woman in his life that he would do anything to protect.

Lilah bravely reached out to Snow, so small and fragile compared with the immense male, and gently laid her hand on his cheek.

Snow instantly calmed, his eyes closing and the sharp spikes of anger emanating from him turning to gentle ripples.

Antoine hadn't moved an inch since roaring. He stood immobile in the middle of the stage, eyes glued on his brother, horror filling them.

Lord and Lady Hallebrand chose that moment to make an ungainly dash for the exit, their son hot on their heels. The two vampires opposite Callum fled too, throwing the stage door open so hard it didn't swing back again.

"Snow?" Antoine said in a soothing tone and the large male vampire looked up at him and huffed like a wild beast. Antoine carefully approached him, crouched at the edge of the stage, and reached through the bars to his older brother.

Snow shifted his cheek to rest in Antoine's large hand and closed his eyes.

"I did not mean to disturb you," Antoine whispered and Callum turned away, leaving him to calm his brother.

He had more important matters to tend to.

The three female werewolves had yet to change back. He approached them. The tan and the brown one moved forwards, snarling and bearing their fangs, their hackles rising again. They were protecting the black one.

All three of them were injured, blood staining their fur. Was the third injured worse than the other two? He couldn't tell. The wolf's fur was so dark it obscured the blood.

"Kristina?" He looked at each wolf in turn. The two at the front growled at him again and took a step forwards, holding their heads low, their ears going backwards. "I am not going to hurt you... any of you."

The black wolf slowly changed, her fur sweeping backwards to reveal pale bloodstained skin as her limbs twisted back into human form. She snarled and whimpered, and then curled up on her side when she had finished her transformation.

"Kristina." Callum reached for her and the other two wolves lunged for him. He backed off again and Kristina pushed herself up, sitting with her legs tucked to one side and her arms crossed over her breasts.

"I had nothing to do with this," he said and she looked at him through her tangled brown hair, her hazel eyes dark and cold. "Please, Kristina. You know me. I only source performers, never victims. None of us knew what was going to happen. We thought they wanted werewolf performers, not people they could treat like animals and abuse."

His stomach turned at the thought of what might have happened if he hadn't returned when he had. The vampires had obviously been ordered to break the werewolves and bring them to their knees before violating them, and possibly killing them. It sickened him.

It was one thing to act out something natural like a vampire hunting a human, feeding on them before an audience, giving the human their pleasure so they felt no pain and creating an illusion of death that would satisfy the vampire audience. It was completely another to violate and abuse a conscious creature, using it for sport and then killing it.

Vampirerotique hadn't killed anyone on stage in years. It was easy to fool the audience into believing the humans died just as they had always done in the past. The scent of blood and sex when combined with the sight of a vampire feeding was enough to make even the strongest, oldest of his kind hazy with hunger and pleasure. All the vampire controlling and feeding on the human had to do was send a command for their heartbeat to slow as far as it could go and the audience were fooled.

It certainly made business a lot cleaner and easier. Everyone was happy. The humans were paid handsomely for their erotic dealings, just as they had been promised, and had their memories of the night wiped, the audience got their high from the blood and the sex and apparent death, and the vampire performers were well fed. No need to dispose of bodies. No conscience nagging him. Just the way he liked it.

"Kristina," he whispered and sank to his knees. "Please believe me. When you disappeared, I didn't know what to do. I looked everywhere for you. I thought you had been taken by those werewolves, and then by your pack. I came here tonight intending to tell Antoine that I would be leaving again straight away to track down your pack and find you."

"You what?" Antoine turned on him and Callum ignored him. He muttered to himself, "I don't need this. Not after Javier."

Callum knew that.

He had openly declared that she was his lover in front of a large group of aristocrats tonight. It would filter through to the others and then down to the elite vampires.

The potential impact on their business was frightening, but not as much as the other problem that firmly settled at the front of his mind, terrifying him.

His parents were going to be paying him a visit when they heard that he had a werewolf lover.

Bringing humans into the family was one thing. A werewolf? He wouldn't be surprised if they disowned him.

And he didn't care.

He would endure it if it meant being with Kristina.

"Kristina," he said, trying to get her attention again. "Let me tend to your wounds. I only want to protect you. I love you, Kristina... and I know you love me."

She cast her gaze downwards, crimson heating her cheeks.

He rose to his feet and stepped towards her. The two female wolves growled again.

"It's fine," Kristina said at last. "He won't hurt me. He means it."

"It damned well is not fine," Antoine muttered and strode to the bent bars.

He slipped through them and hopped down onto the red carpet. He took Snow from Javier and led his brother out of the theatre.

Javier looked over at Callum, smiled, and led Lilah out too.

Callum wasn't going to celebrate the fact that Antoine hadn't killed him, not just yet. He was sure that the older more powerful vampire would be requesting his presence in his office soon enough. He would face him when the time came, but right now he had to tend to Kristina and the other two females. They changed back, covering themselves with their hands.

He picked up the black velvet cage cover and tore it into three pieces. The two women took all three pieces from him, the blonde wrapping one around Kristina's shoulders as she stood.

"Are you hurt?" He waited with bated breath for her response.

With all the blood on her, it was hard to tell whether any of her wounds were serious, or whether it was just shallow cuts and the rest was blood from the vampires.

She shook her head. "Nothing more than scratches... just a little shaken up."

He wanted to track down the vampires who had done this to her and butcher them for that reason alone. Fear still lingered in her scent and in her blood within him. He resisted his need to reach out to her and touch her, to comfort himself and soothe his anger by feeling her and confirming that she was alright.

He looked at the other two werewolves.

"What about you?"

They still looked wary of him but both of them shook their heads. He walked towards Kristina and he half expected them to snarl again and force him away.

"I have a car outside." Callum looked from her to the two female werewolves. "I will take you all to The Langham, all expenses paid of course, and will see to everything for you. I can't make up for what happened to you here... but I can promise that you will all be safe there."

The two females didn't look as though they were going to accept such an offer from a man obviously involved with the theatre that had almost got them killed.

Kristina stepped past them and held her hand out to him.

Relief beat through him and he slipped his hand under hers, closed his fingers around it, and sighed.

It felt so good to touch her again.

He drew her into his embrace and held her close, wrapping her carefully in his arms, reassuring himself that she was safe now.

He didn't care what the future held for them, or how angry Antoine was or how his parents would react to the news that he had fallen in love with a werewolf.

He only cared that Kristina was safe.

"I love you," he whispered close to her ear, aware that the two females were watching them and listening. He tangled his fingers in her wavy hair and leaned into her.

Kristina tipped her head back, so her cheek pressed against his, and wrapped her arms around his neck. "I love you too."

Callum closed his eyes and sighed, warmth filling him and urging him to make her say it again. He didn't get a chance. She spoke before he could.

"We'll need suites." Kristina drew back and looked thoughtful, a wicked glint in her eyes. The sight of it reassured him more than anything she could have said. She was safe and unharmed, and wasn't going to run away from him, but he was certain that she was going to make him and Vampirerotique pay handsomely for what had happened to her and her companions. "The best suites, and the best food, and the finest clothes, and no check out date... and the name of the bastards who set this up."

He opened his eyes and looked at the two women. Their yellowing eyes held his, feral and dangerous, conveying their feelings perfectly. They wanted revenge too.

"Whatever my ladies want, my ladies will receive... including a vampire bodyguard. I will track the vampires with you and we'll deal with them together. I want their blood for this too."

Kristina nodded. The two women echoed her agreement. He wrapped his arm around her slender shoulders and led her from the stage, the two women following them.

Vengeance would have to wait.

First he had to tend to Kristina and her fellow werewolves, ensuring their injuries were seen to and that they felt safe again and on their way to recovering from their ordeal.

"I have your belongings," he said and she glanced up at him.

"You really were looking for me," she whispered and he nodded.

"I went crazy without you, Kristina. I had to find you and had to have you in my arms again. I came back intent on heading straight out to track down your pack and face your alpha. I never expected I would find you here. I'm only glad I got here when I did. I wish I had got here sooner." His voice cracked as images of what might have been flickered across his eyes and he squeezed them shut, trying to push them away.

He was sure that Antoine would have stopped it if he hadn't been here to do so himself. Antoine had seemed genuinely distressed by what he had witnessed on stage before the act had turned sickening. When the veil had lifted to reveal the three werewolves, Callum had felt the spike in his anger that pushed it into the volcanic zone. The vampires were lucky that Antoine hadn't lost it and butchered them all.

Kristina leaned her head against Callum's chest, bringing him back to her. "You got here in time, and that was all that mattered. You did a bad thing tonight didn't you?"

Callum nodded. Antoine would be making sure he knew that soon enough.

"I don't care what those vampires think... I don't even care what Javier, Snow and Antoine think of me. They can punish me all they want. All that matters is that I love you, and that you're safe now, back in my arms." He smiled down at her when she stopped and looked up into his eyes, her hazel ones full of warmth and affection. "You're addictive... the feel of you, your touch, your kiss, your smile... the sound of your voice and how you feel in my arms when we're sleeping together. I crave you."

She smiled. "I crave something too."

"Me?" he said.

Her smile turned wicked. "That's a given. I've spent a week with you and can't get you out of my system... and now I plan on going to that no doubt fancy hotel you mentioned and keeping you all to myself for a week or maybe five."

"Or maybe forever." Those words came out before he could consider the consequences.

Kristina tensed and so did the two females behind him.

It wasn't everyday that a vampire voiced an intention to spend the rest of his life with a werewolf but that was what he was doing, and now that it was out there, he felt lighter inside, as though a weight had lifted from his heart.

Her smile was all the answer he needed. It was brilliant and dazzling.

"Or maybe forever," she echoed and pressed a quick kiss to his lips. He wrapped his arm around her again, warm from head to toe. "But you know what I really crave?"

"What?" he brushed a kiss over her hair and had the feeling the food bill at the hotel was going to be even higher than the cost of the rooms and clothing combined.

"Bacon and eggs," she said and he smiled.

They walked a little further through the theatre, heading for the foyer. That was a small list of food for his werewolf. Something told him she wasn't finished. He glanced at her out of the corner of his eye. She grinned to herself, eyes lighting up, and rubbed her stomach.

"No... I really want pancakes, and waffles, with strawberries and cream and chocolate sauce. With a milkshake. Banana flavoured... and a tropical smoothie."

Callum looked over his shoulder at the two females behind him, trying to see if this was typical werewolf behaviour and they were thinking about all the food they wanted too.

They were staring at the back of Kristina's head, strange smiles on their faces, as though they were in on a joke and he and Kristina weren't.

"And I want bacon in the smoothie... and oh... I want onions... and beetroot, together. Can I have some beetroot? Beetroot onion ice-cream."

Each step closer to the limousine he took, her list of food she craved became stranger and the temperature turned colder around Callum, until he was barely moving.

Craving.

He looked down at her hand on the black velvet covering her stomach, recounted the list of bizarre things she wanted to eat, recalled that female humans had such behaviour during certain times, and then the way the two female werewolves had been protecting her on stage.

He looked back at the werewolves.

They smiled at him.

His eyes widened.

He swallowed hard.

Kristina smiled brightly at him. "What's wrong?"

He frowned and thought about how to broach the subject. It seemed impossible. He told himself that was because it was. To prove it, he placed his hand over hers and focused his senses on her stomach, staring at it and feeling beyond their hands.

"Callum?" she said and at that moment, he felt the tiny pulse of life within her.

Her eyes shot wide.

"It isn't possible," they said in unison.

"It most certainly is." The blonde werewolf pushed the door to the foyer open.

The brunette nodded in agreement and placed her hand on Kristina's shoulder before passing her. "I've seen it before."

Callum stared down into Kristina's eyes.

The shock in them faded and then she dropped her gaze to her stomach and their joined hands.

Callum linked their fingers, silently showing her that she didn't have to be afraid. He would stay with her through everything, would remain at her side and would raise their child with her.

He had never thought about a family before, but he couldn't think of anyone else in the world he would rather start one with than Kristina.

"Whatever happens," he said and she met his gaze again. "This is proof of our love for each other. I will do all I can to be a good father, and a good mate for you, Kristina. We will raise our child together, surrounded by our love, so it will never feel like an outcast. It will know that love between our species is possible. Be my mate, Kristina... my wife... and I will be your husband."

She smiled, threw herself into his arms and kissed him. "Yes."

Callum held her close, swept her up into his arms so he was cradling her, and carried her towards the car.

"Now, let's see what we can do about getting you a suite and all that food you're craving," he said.

She grinned up at him. “I’ve changed my mind. I want something else now.”

He looked down at her and raised a single eyebrow.

“I have an intense craving for you.”

Callum growled and kissed her.

He could satisfy that craving.

He would spend the next week satisfying it and every desire she had, making love to her from dusk until dawn, and then sleeping with her in his arms.

And then when the week was done, he would do it all over, and then repeat it again.

Forever.

The End

Read on for a preview of the next book in the London Vampires romance series, Seduce!

SEDUCE

Sera's attention wasn't on the show.

While her sire sat beside her in the sumptuous red velvet seats of the dark stalls, her focus fixed on the erotic acts playing out on the stage of Vampirerotique, Sera's gaze was elsewhere, drawn to a man who had been on her mind since the first time she had set eyes on him over a year ago.

He stood to her right at the edge of the theatre near the front row, shadows clinging to him as though they too were drawn to his lethal beauty, his own gaze on the stage.

Not once did it stray from the performance—not even when she prayed under her breath every second that it would come to rest on her—and never did the intensity of it lessen.

His pale icy eyes scrutinised everything, watching closely, as though he was studying it so he could give a blow-by-blow description of it to someone after it had ended.

Perhaps he did.

He often disappeared as soon as the show reached its climax with the bloodletting, heading through the double doors that led backstage to an area she could only imagine.

Her sire, Elizabeth, had described it for her a few times but she had always been more interested in learning more about the enigma that was the vampire who ran the theatre.

Antoine.

His name was as exotic as his looks. The deadly combination of lush chocolate brown hair, those intense pale blue eyes and his lithe figure that just screamed he would look like a god naked, was too much for her. The more she saw him, the more she wanted him.

Regardless of the warnings that her sire often whispered in her ear.

"Perhaps I should arrange for a seat closer to him next time?" Elizabeth hissed across at her, amusement ringing in her tone.

Sera tore her eyes away from Antoine, ashamed that she wasn't watching the show that had cost her sire a pretty penny. Elizabeth had been getting her better seats with each performance and Sera knew that the closer they were to the stage and the action, the more expensive the tickets became.

Not only that, but she had paid for Sera's new outfit of a lacy deep green camisole top that matched her eyes and tight black jeans that showed off her legs to perfection, and the new highlights in her long blonde hair as well as the makeover they had both enjoyed this evening before attending the theatre.

She tried to watch the show, concentrated hard on maintaining her focus on the act playing out on the black stage but she couldn't take in any of it. Her head swam, unable to keep track of what was happening, focus diverted by the drop-dead-gorgeous man who stood barely twenty feet away from her. She gritted her teeth and frowned, forcing her eyes to follow the performers. It didn't help.

Seats closer to the stage just meant closer to Antoine, presenting her with a much better view of him. A view she didn't want to squander.

Her gaze drifted back to him as though he had his own gravity and she was powerless against its pull. He stood side on to her, his tailored black trousers and crisp charcoal shirt accentuating his figure, igniting her imagination.

It raced to picture him naked.

Long legs and powerful thighs. Firm buttocks with sexy dimples above them. A lean muscled back that followed the sensual curve of his spine and flowed into strong shoulders that would be a pleasure to study as he moved. And finally, a chiselled torso blessed with rope after rope of honed muscles down his stomach and a chest that would feel solid beneath her cheek and palm as he held her protectively in his embrace.

Elizabeth giggled, the sound so out of place during the intense erotic performance that the dark-haired man in front of them looked over his shoulder and frowned.

"You don't want to get involved with him. It wouldn't end well," Elizabeth said.

Sera wished that her sire had waited for the man to turn away before saying that. Now he was frowning at them both, dark eyebrows drawn tight above red eyes.

Elizabeth dismissively waved her hand, long scarlet nails catching the bright colourful lights that illuminated the stage. "I'm not talking about you. You'll miss one of the best bits."

The man's frown hardened but he turned back to the show. Elizabeth swept her wavy dark red hair over her shoulder and returned her attention to the performance too. Sera fidgeted on her seat when she caught a glimpse of the man on stage.

Victor.

Elizabeth had worked with him during her time at the London theatre.

He had been with Vampirerotique since a few years after it had opened a century ago and was their star performer. The large brunet male was currently pumping a woman in centre stage, his fangs enormous as he growled and fucked her side on to the audience so they could witness the whole act.

The petite brunette bent over in front of him was moaning with each deep plunge of his cock, her hands grasping her knees and breasts swinging in time with his powerful thrusts.

Two other men were pleasuring human females a short distance from him. The men sat on the red velvet gold-framed couches, one on each, flanking Victor where he stood close to the front of the black stage. The human females under the thrall of the other two vampires were facing the audience, kneeling astride the one who controlled them, bouncing on his cock and groaning as they palmed their breasts.

Sera looked away, cheeks burning.

Elizabeth leaned towards her. "Besides, he's as frigid as a nun and as cold as ice. In the fifty years that I worked for him, I never once saw him with a woman. The only person he loves is his messed up brother, and that's one relationship you don't want to interfere with."

Sera had heard the warnings so many times now that they were losing their effect. Every time Elizabeth brought her to the theatre to watch a performance, she reiterated the long list of reasons why Sera shouldn't want Antoine.

Unfortunately, those warnings only made her want him even more. According to Elizabeth, the gorgeous male vampire had been alone for God only knew how long. Sera wanted to be the woman to smash his armour and tear down his defences, and end his loneliness.

If he was lonely.

Her gaze slid back to Antoine. He stood rod straight, posture perfect, shoulders tipped back as he continued to study the performance. The first few times she had seen him, she hadn't thought to ask her sire about him.

She had thought he was just one of the crowd stretching his legs. When Elizabeth had noticed her staring, she had told her that he was one of the owners of the theatre, and an aristocrat vampire. That had explained the tilt of his chin and the air of pride he wore, and perhaps even the coldness that settled on his face at times when he was greeting the more important guests before the show started.

He was so distant, even looked miles away as he studied the show, lost in thoughts that she wanted to know.

Elizabeth nudged her and she looked back at the stage, trying to keep her eyes off Antoine. If she couldn't recount at least half of what had happened, Elizabeth would give her an earful on their way back to the city centre apartment they shared.

Things were heating up on stage. Victor had finished with his vampire female and was now toying with one of the humans, a young redhead with full breasts.

The blond male vampire that had been with the female on the couch was with them, kissing her as Victor stood behind her, palming her breasts and rubbing himself against her backside. The blond male looked into her eyes and she turned obediently in his arms, coming to face Victor.

She stared at him. Or beyond him.

Her glassy expression said that the male now behind her wasn't lessening any of his control just yet.

It felt so wrong to watch a woman under the power of a vampire, unable to do anything to disobey her temporary master, but she couldn't deny that it turned her on a little. The woman wouldn't know any discomfort or panic. She was so deep under that she was probably experiencing the purest hit of pleasure she had ever had. Exactly what she had signed on for.

Elizabeth had let Sera in on a secret.

Apparently, all of the humans who participated in the shows had agreed to the erotic acts in exchange for a rather handsome amount of money.

Elizabeth said it hadn't always been that way, but modern times called for a modern approach, and it was far easier not to kill them. The humans knew they would be participating in an on-stage orgy for an audience, and most of them had done such acts before, they just didn't know what they shared that stage with.

Vampires.

That meant they also didn't know they would be doing things under hypnosis.

Not that many of the humans required hypnosis to make them fully participate. The blond male vampire had lessened his control over the redheaded female human bent over in front of him, letting her desire rule her instead, and she was moaning and writhing against him, rubbing herself against his long hard cock.

Sera stared, cheeks heating, as he slowly inched his erection into her body and Victor stepped up in front of the woman. She reached for his rigid cock and closed her eyes as she wrapped her lips around his full length, swallowing him each time he thrust into her mouth.

The man behind her pumped her at the same pace, drawn out and deep, slow enough that the audience was twitching for more.

Sera stared at the blond male, imagining Antoine behind her like that, his face a picture of pleasure as he slid in and out with long deep strokes.

Her gaze shot back to the man of her fantasy and she found he was still staring at the stage with the usual detached look on his face, as though the sight of two men on one woman didn't arouse him in the slightest. She supposed that he had probably seen enough shows that he was immune to their effect now.

A few impatient growls erupted through the theatre and he flicked a glance over the audience and then went back to watching the show.

Sera had tried to talk to him once, when he had passed her by after the show had ended with the feeding and the crowd were leaving.

He had blanked her.

He hadn't even glanced her way. He had walked straight past her as though she didn't exist. She had spoken loudly enough that he must have heard her. It was after that moment that Elizabeth had started with the warnings, revealing only a tantalising amount of information about the powerful handsome aristocrat, just enough to make Sera want him even more.

Now, she craved his eyes on her, wanted to hear him speak and know his voice at last, and above all, she wanted to look up into his eyes and try to see past the barriers around his heart so she could understand him.

Was his distance from everyone just because he was an aristocrat, or was there more to it than that?

A shriek from the stage melted into a moan of pleasure and the smell of human blood spilled through the air, encompassing her.

Antoine visibly tensed, his arms flexing beneath his charcoal tailored shirt, as though he had clenched his fists. His pale eyes darkened, changed just as hers did to reveal her true nature. He turned away and she feared he would leave earlier than usual and her chance would slip by once again.

She tugged on Elizabeth's arm and her sire sighed, rose to her feet, briefly applauded and then started along the row with her trailing behind. Her legs bumped several vampires who were still trying to watch the final act, absorbing the scent and the thrill of bloodshed. She didn't care for it herself. More important matters needed her attention.

The men and women she passed snarled at her, baring their fangs in her direction and leaning to one side in an attempt to see past her. She muttered her apologies, trying to move quickly so they didn't attack her. Elizabeth made that impossible. She moved slowly and with grace in her long scarlet dress, her head held high and no apologies leaving her lips.

Her sire was old enough to stand against these vampires should they choose to attack but Sera wasn't. It would be years before she had the strength of her sire. They reached the last person and broke out onto the wide strip of red carpet that lined the edge of the theatre.

"Antoine," Elizabeth called and he paused and swung back to face her.

Sera's heart almost stopped when his deep crimson gaze briefly flickered to her before returning to her sire.

Her nerves rose as he strolled up the incline to meet Elizabeth and Sera slowed, the gap between her and Elizabeth growing larger by the second.

What was she doing?

It had taken months for her to convince her sire to do this for her and now that she had finally agreed, her nerve was going to fail? She wanted this man's eyes on her, wanted to be alone with him, and the only way to get what she wanted was to get a job at the theatre.

If she made it past the interview, then Antoine would have to meet with her.

Elizabeth had said that he spoke with each new performer to ensure they were suitable for the theatre.

Sera just had to get the interview out of the way and then she would have the chance she wanted.

Once they were alone in his office, she would take a shot at convincing Antoine that she was the woman for him. Whatever the outcome of that meeting was, she would quit her role as a performer. She didn't intend to perform at the theatre.

Hell, no.

She didn't have the right sort of personality for that. She wanted to blush whenever she chanced a glance at the black and red stage set and saw what the couples on it were doing. If it weren't for Antoine's presence in the theatre and her sire's insistence that they have a little fun, she would never come to such a place.

"Callum," a deep male voice called out, sharp with authority, and Sera stopped dead.

Sweet mercy, Antoine had a voice that could tame even the wildest of angels.

That voice was a drug.

It went straight into her heart and raced through her veins, the effect sweeter than any amount of blood.

Sera turned towards her sire and Antoine, only to see that he was walking away, leaving her sire with another dark-haired man.

He was handsome, full of smiles as he spoke to Elizabeth, far warmer and more amiable than Antoine was but nowhere near as alluring. Elizabeth signalled her to join them and she did, moving past the vampires now spilling out of the stalls and watching Antoine leave at the same time.

She'd had a chance to meet him and she had blown it.

If she had only kept up with her sire, she would have been close to him, maybe would have caught his attention this time and had his eyes on her at last.

"Is this her?" the vampire called Callum said and ran a glance over her.

Sera kept still, feeling as though she was for sale as he moved around her, his eyes on her body, inspecting and scrutinising every inch.

He came back to stand before her and looked at Elizabeth. "The summer season will end soon so we'll have time to train her before the winter one begins but we need someone with natural talent. Does she have what it takes?"

Sera opened her mouth to speak but Elizabeth beat her to it.

"Absolutely. She's my child, Cal. It's all in the blood." Elizabeth smiled broadly at him, red lips curving perfectly. Her deep brown eyes shone with warmth and she swept her dark red hair over her shoulders, exposing their bare curves. "You know I am one of your best ever performers."

Callum nodded and the longer lengths of his cropped black hair fell down over one emerald green eye. He frowned and raked it back, and then ran a hand around the nape of his neck, drawing Sera's eyes to a set of dark marks on it.

A bite mark.

It looked deep and fresh too, no more than a night or two old.

Did he have a lover?

He looked at her again and Sera's gaze leapt to his.

She swallowed the desire to confess that her sire was lying and she had no natural talent for the sort of thing that he was talking about. She smiled instead, trying to look every bit as seductive as her sire. Elizabeth had been Vampirerotique's star female performer until she had decided to quit her job and return to her family instead. They had met shortly after that, and Elizabeth had turned her into a vampire. That was thirty years ago now. It had taken Sera most of those years to become accustomed to life as a vampire.

"Come by tomorrow night when we're closed," Callum said. "Now, if you'll excuse me."

"Thank you," Sera said and he smiled at her, nodded, and then disappeared into the crowd.

Their excited chatter filled the theatre, the people passing her by discussing the show and the finale. Other elite vampires were still in their seats, enjoying the lingering scent of blood and sharing an intimate moment of their own with their partners. Sometimes the kissing that happened post-performance in the stalls was more erotic than what occurred on stage.

Sera dragged her gaze away from one couple near the front who were going at it with wild abandon. They looked as though they wouldn't make it out of the theatre before they succumbed to their desire and took things a step further.

She glanced out of the corner of her eye at Elizabeth. "Does Callum have a lover?"

"I thought you had set your sights on Antoine?" Elizabeth laughed when she blushed and then her expression darkened. "A wife... and I've heard rumours that she's a werewolf."

A werewolf? Sera had expected the owners of an erotic theatre to be quite liberal and wild, but marrying a werewolf? She definitely hadn't expected that one.

"You're serious?" She never could tell with her sire.

The woman enjoyed a joke more than was natural. Sera supposed that you needed to have an easygoing attitude when you chose to spend fifty years participating in an on-stage orgy with people you hardly knew.

Her stomach turned.

Thank the Devil she wouldn't have to do such a thing to get her chance to speak with Antoine. Just an interview that she would ace thanks to her sire's tuition and then she would be in his office, alone with him. Just the thought stirred heat in her veins.

Since her sire had agreed to help her, she had spent every night trying to figure out how to win Antoine.

It wasn't going to be easy. She knew that much.

She'd had lovers in her human life and even in her vampire one, but she had never pursued a man before, not as she intended to with Antoine.

Elizabeth had laughed when she had confessed that and had told her that she should probably start with easier prey and work her way up to someone like Antoine. That gave her the feeling that she was going to fail.

What sort of woman would he desire?

He ran an erotic theatre and watched the beautiful women performing on his stage without the barest hint of desire in his expression. If they couldn't arouse him, what hope did she have?

Maybe he wasn't interested in women who worked at his theatre. If that was the case, was she only shooting down what slim chance she had with him by interviewing for a position as a performer?

"I need a drink, and you look as though you could use one too." Elizabeth grasped her wrist and tugged her towards the exit at the back of the theatre. "Come along, my pupil. You have a lot to learn before tomorrow night if you're going to have a snowball's chance in Hell of impressing that man."

Sera trudged along behind her sire, weaving through the lingering crowd. Elizabeth's warnings rang in her ears, one louder than the rest.

She glanced up at the three storeys of elegant boxes that lined the theatre. The gold on the carvings decorating the curved cream low walls that edged the private boxes reflected the warm lights that illuminated the heavy red velvet curtain now closed across the stage. Matching curtains hung at the back of the boxes, some of them open now that the performance had ended. Many of the boxes were empty but beautifully dressed ladies and gentlemen still occupied the others.

She spotted Antoine amongst a group in one of the boxes on the first tier. He was smiling. She had never seen him smile. It looked forced to her.

Hollow.

Even among his own kind, he was still distant, his eyes devoid of emotion as he put on a grand performance of his own.

Sera wasn't going to overcome the challenge of winning Antoine's heart just by meeting the man.

First, she had to break through a barrier that was beginning to look impenetrable.

He was an aristocrat, and an old one at that. Although he looked barely a day over thirty-five, he was in fact over a thousand years old. His brother, Snow, was almost twice his age.

Sera was an elite.

To an aristocrat, she was some sort of filth they scraped off their shoes and nothing made that clearer than the theatres. The aristocrats sat in their boxes, looking down on the elite gathered in the stalls, separated and distant from those they saw as commoners and mongrels.

That disdain for her kind was the reason why Antoine looked so glacial whenever he had to greet the more important members of the elite, and why he had failed to hear her when she had tried to speak with him. He wanted nothing to do with the elite vampires outside the small circle that were part of the theatre.

He would certainly want nothing to do with her.

Not only was she an elite, but she was a turned human.

She was the bottom rung of the social ladder and he was the top.

The elite that he deemed worthy of a moment of his time, that he greeted with gritted teeth in order to maintain good relations with her kind, were all born as vampires into families that had turned humans within their ranks. None of them were turned humans themselves.

Even Elizabeth was born of a vampire father and turned mother.

If Sera wanted to shatter Antoine's armour, she would have to convince him to see beyond the fact that she was a turned human.

Elizabeth had taught her a few things, weapons that she hadn't held in her arsenal before, but she wasn't sure if she was brave enough to risk using them on Antoine.

Could she do what Elizabeth had said it would take to shatter his defences?

Could she really seduce such a powerful man?

Sera curled her fingers into tight fists and stared at him. He paused in the middle of saying something to the aristocrat vampires in the box with him, slowly turned towards her and then lowered his eyes. They locked on her.

He had felt her watching him.

Her heart beat harder, thumping against her chest as her blood heated, but she held his gaze across the theatre stalls, refusing to back down.

The next time she saw him, she would be alone with him.

And she would seduce him.

SEDUCE

Bloodlust runs in his veins, a dark master waiting for the day it will reign over him. Now a woman with a pure soul and wicked intentions has him in her sights and is determined to crack the ice around his heart, and she might save or damn him.

Antoine stands apart from the world around him, a dangerous and broken soul who must maintain rigid control at all times or risk his dark addiction finally seizing hold of him. The shadows of his past haunt him and he sees his bleak future each night when his brother wakes screaming, his blood addiction turning him savage. He cannot allow himself to feel, but when Sera walks into Vampirerotique, the erotic theatre he runs with three other vampires, to audition, she awakens dangerous desires in him—hungers that could spell the end of both of them.

Sera has wanted Antoine since the night she first saw the gorgeous aristocrat vampire. She can't ignore the deep carnal hunger he stirs in her or the ache to know the heat of his touch. With the help of her sire, an ex-performer at Vampirerotique, she sets in motion a game of seduction, one designed to thaw the ice in Antoine's veins and make him burn for her.

When Sera discovers the shocking truth about his past and the darkness that lurks within him, will she be strong enough to seize his heart with both hands and win him forever or will she lose him to the ghosts that still haunt him?

ABOUT THE AUTHOR

Felicity Heaton is a New York Times and USA Today best-selling author who writes passionate paranormal romance books. In her books she creates detailed worlds, twisting plots, mind-blowing action, intense emotion and heart-stopping romances with leading men that vary from dark deadly vampires to sexy shape-shifters and wicked werewolves, to sinful angels and hot demons!

If you're a fan of paranormal romance authors Lara Adrian, J R Ward, Sherrilyn Kenyon, Kresley Cole, Gena Showalter, Larissa Ione and Christine Feehan then you will enjoy her books too.

If you love your angels a little dark and wicked, her best-selling Her Angel romance series is for you. If you like strong, powerful, and dark vampires then try the Vampires Realm romance series or any of her stand alone vampire romance books. If you're looking for vampire romances that are sinful, passionate and erotic then try her London Vampires romance series. Or if you like hot-blooded alpha heroes who will let nothing stand in the way of them claiming their destined woman then try her Eternal Mates series. It's packed with sexy heroes in a world populated by elves, vampires, fae, demons, shifters, and more. If sexy Greek gods with incredible powers battling to save our world and their home in the Underworld are more your thing, then be sure to step into the world of Guardians of Hades.

If you have enjoyed this story, please take a moment to contact the author at **author@felicityheaton.com** or to post a review of the book online

Connect with Felicity:
Website – http://www.felicityheaton.com
Blog – http://www.felicityheaton.com/blog/
Twitter – http://twitter.com/felicityheaton
Facebook – http://www.facebook.com/felicityheaton
Goodreads – http://www.goodreads.com/felicityheaton
Mailing List – http://www.felicityheaton.com/newsletter.php

FIND OUT MORE ABOUT HER BOOKS AT:
http://www.felicityheaton.com

Printed in Great Britain
by Amazon